T0245788

EIDOLON: THE AURIC HAMMER

Further reading from The Horus Heresy

THE HORUS HERESY®

Book 1 – HORUS RISING
Dan Abnett

Book 2 – FALSE GODS
Graham McNeill

Book 3 – GALAXY IN FLAMES
Ben Counter

Book 4 – THE FLIGHT OF
THE EISENSTEIN
James Swallow

___THE HORUS HERESY*___
SIEGE OF TERRA

Book 1 – THE SOLAR WAR
John French

Book 2 – THE LOST AND
THE DAMNED
Guy Haley

Book 3 – THE FIRST WALL
Gav Thorpe

Book 4 – SATURNINE
Dan Abnett

Book 5 – MORTIS
John French

Book 6 – WARHAWK
Chris Wraight

Book 7 – ECHOES OF ETERNITY
Aaron Dembski-Bowden

Book 8 – THE END AND THE DEATH:
VOLUME I
Dan Abnett

Book 8 – THE END AND THE DEATH:
VOLUME II
Dan Abnett

Book 8 – THE END AND THE DEATH:
VOLUME III
Dan Abnett

SONS OF THE SELENAR (Novella)
Graham McNeill

FURY OF MAGNUS (Novella)
Graham McNeill

GARRO: KNIGHT OF GREY (Novella)
James Swallow

THE HORUS HERESY®
PRIMARCHS

ANGRON:
SLAVE OF NUCERIA
Ian St. Martin

KONRAD CURZE:
THE NIGHT HAUNTER
Guy Haley

LION EL'JONSON:
LORD OF THE FIRST
David Guymer

ALPHARIUS:
HEAD OF THE HYDRA
Mike Brooks

The Horus Heresy Character Series

VALDOR:
BIRTH OF THE IMPERIUM
Chris Wraight

LUTHER:
FIRST OF THE FALLEN
Gav Thorpe

SIGISMUND:
THE ETERNAL CRUSADER
John French

EIDOLON:
THE AURIC HAMMER
Marc Collins

*Order the full range of Horus Heresy novels, audio dramas and audiobooks
from* blacklibrary.com

EIDOLON: THE AURIC HAMMER

MARC COLLINS

BLACK LIBRARY

A BLACK LIBRARY PUBLICATION

First published in 2024.
This edition published in Great Britain in 2024 by
Black Library, Games Workshop Ltd., Willow Road,
Nottingham, NG7 2WS, UK.

Represented by: Games Workshop Limited – Irish branch,
Unit 3, Lower Liffey Street, Dublin 1,
D01 K199, Ireland.

10 9 8 7 6 5 4 3 2 1

Produced by Games Workshop in Nottingham.
Cover illustration by Mauro Belfiore.

A CIP record for this book is available from the British Library.

ISBN 13: 978-1-80407-352-0

See Black Library on the internet at

blacklibrary.com

Find out more about Games Workshop
and the worlds of Warhammer at

games-workshop.com

Printed and bound in China.

For Briana, Kirsty and Rachael. With all the excesses of my heart.

WARHAMMER®
THE HORUS HERESY

It is a time of legend.

Mighty heroes battle for the right to rule the galaxy.
The vast armies of the Emperor of Mankind conquer
the stars in a Great Crusade – the myriad alien races
are to be smashed by His elite warriors and wiped
from the face of history.

The dawn of a new age of supremacy for humanity
beckons. Gleaming citadels of marble and gold celebrate
the many victories of the Emperor, as system after
system is brought back under His control. Triumphs are
raised on a million worlds to record the epic deeds of
His most powerful champions.

First and foremost amongst these are the primarchs,
superhuman beings who have led the Space Marine
Legions in campaign after campaign. They are
unstoppable and magnificent, the pinnacle of the
Emperor's genetic experimentation, while the Space
Marines themselves are the mightiest human warriors
the galaxy has ever known, each capable of besting a
hundred normal men or more in combat.

Many are the tales told of these legendary beings.
From the halls of the Imperial Palace on Terra to the
outermost reaches of Ultima Segmentum, their deeds
are known to be shaping the very future of the galaxy.
But can such souls remain free of doubt and corruption
forever? Or will the temptation of greater power prove
too much for even the most loyal sons of the Emperor?

The seeds of heresy have already been sown, and the
start of the greatest war in the history of mankind is
but a few years away...

'We are, all of us, seekers after truth. Illumination comes only through unity, through the singular pursuit of absolute perfection. We carry it up from the dust of worlds once thought dead: Terra and Chemos. We raise them up to the stars. I say to you now, the galaxy deserves but one master. One path and one purpose. When we have ensured that, when we have restored unity to what has been set asunder, only then will humanity inherit a perfect cosmos.'

– Attributed to the primarch Fulgrim,
at the Liberation of Tatricala

ACT ONE

MIND

ONE

———————————————

In the days before their illumination, it had been taken as a certainty by the warriors who waged the Great Crusade that ships could not be haunted by spirits. Not truly. The Mechanicum preached of it, of course, and void sailors kept their own atrophied superstitions, but to the warriors-elect of the Legiones Astartes, to the peerless brotherhood of the III Legion, such things were laughable myths from a bygone age.

Now, through the corridors of the *Wage of Sin*, madness stalked.

The transit from Ullanor had not been easy or without incident. The ships of the fleet had grown insular and febrile, their hulls rippling like tormented flesh. Suicides, already common amongst the mortal herd, had become endemic. The warriors of the III, beyond such mortal weakness, were restless and distant – haunted by whatever force moved through the great vessel like a predator king, determined to find and seize its heart.

Haunted. The thought itself seemed anathema. Yet there were
ghosts in the machines, knifing through the ether-streaked void to
prey upon the ships of the flotilla. The impossible and the unthink-
able had become all too common. The time of their naivety in
the face of the galaxy's true nature was long behind them. It had
changed around them, almost without them being aware of it.

Time, Lord Commander Primus Eidolon reflected, had changed
so many things.

He was not the same being who had set out upon the Great
Crusade's vulgar path of conquest. Though he had passed through
the trials to make him a child of the Legion, a true son of the
Phoenix, it was the years of the new war that had altered him in
the most fundamental of ways.

Eidolon had been beautiful once, sharing in the genetic splendour passed down from his primarch. It was a supreme irony,
then, that Fulgrim himself had robbed him of it. The scar across
Eidolon's throat had healed badly, a wound inflicted as much
upon his soul as on his flesh. Even as his neck pulsed with the
sonic alterations conferred by the Chief Apothecary, the scar
remained resolutely unbending. It flexed and constricted with
every fitful motion, restricting the lord commander's full range
of motion. His skin was bloodlessly pale, his eyes now cataracted and rheumy. His hair fell down one side of his head,
lank and wilted like dead plant growth.

Yes, he had been beautiful, once… but that had been long
ago and taken at a demigod's whim.

*Fitting, is it not? Jealousy was always one of your many flaws,
father.*

Eidolon bit away the thought. It was unbecoming, both of
him and of Fulgrim. The daemonic presence of the Primarch
Ascendant, the Phoenix-in-his-Apotheosis, lingered amidst the
corridors of his ship. In the aftermath of Ullanor's bleak council,
it would not do to tempt Fulgrim's attentions.

Not when there were other matters clawing at Eidolon's mind. Stalked and tormented as he was. *Haunted,* he thought again.

Something cooed and whispered at his ear, and he leant his head back, drumming it against the command throne as though pain could dismiss the threat. It lolled this way and that with every pulse of his throat, like a child's marionette, over-balanced and caricatured. Whatever drifted about him, coiling and writhing just beneath reality's skin, was close enough to touch him. He was braced to feel claws tease his skin in lines of fire, for fangs to close around his throat.

After so long being hunted… perhaps the culmination would be nothing short of a delight. Eidolon yearned to savour the experience.

Around him, the command bridge of the *Wage of Sin* rose in tarnished splendour. Like its master it had once been a beautiful thing; now it was exalted, transformed by the III Legion's unleashed appetites. Banners of human skin fluttered from the iron ribs of its ceiling, and mirrors glimmered in broken majesty from the corners of the room, casting forth reflections that should not exist – images which moved too slowly, or too quickly, or watched their subjects when they were not looking. Sometimes Eidolon would catch a shattered image's eye as it leered and laughed at him with his own face. An incarnate mockery. Eidolon could have sworn he'd heard derision drifting about him as the shattered reflection judged and assessed him. He shook himself, banished the memory, and rolled his shoulders.

'Status report,' he rumbled, rising from his command throne. Harvested bone glistened wetly along its edges, shimmering with an internal light that caught on the lines of Eidolon's corroded, ruined armour.

His hand contracted again, reaching across to the arm of his throne, stroking the haft of the thunder hammer that reclined there. *Glory Aeterna* was a weapon of consummate craft, one he had wielded with skill and devotion ever since the primarch had graced him with it. He turned from it and spoke to the empty air.

'Now we know our purpose,' he breathed. 'At last the galaxy will understand as we have been made to.' He blinked, milky eyes darting with the sudden need for stimulus. 'Status report!' he called again. He was not sure whether he had slipped so deeply into his reverie that he had missed the report or whether those creatures still at their posts had simply ignored him, lost to their own mania.

Either way, it was an inexcusable lapse for someone of his position.

'Fleet disposition holds, esteemed lord,' crooned what passed for the vessel's master of auspex. The androgynous thing had no eyes, only sutured sockets where they had once rested. A web of cables were wired and screwed into its back, forcing sensor data into its nervous system in an unceasing wave of cognitive feedback and neural overload. The creature mewled and writhed, caught in the ecstasy of complete surrender to excess and duty. Somewhere, behind the chorus of muted pleasure, Eidolon could hear someone sniggering. 'Responses from the *Sublime Blade* and the *Broken Monarch*, the *Dwell Eternal* and *His Beauty Manifest*. The auxiliary transport ships are in transit as well. The disposition of the Third Millennial holds true, my lord.'

The Third Millennial. He smiled. That was the command he had taken for his own, upon the road to Terra. Mere rabble, soon to stand as gods upon the Throneworld's burning skin.

Such a ripe harvest. They could be so much more. We could–

'Excellent,' Eidolon said, forcing himself to ignore the sound of mockery, and reached out to stroke the inlaid jewels along one osseus arm of his throne, the gems winking in the garish lights. Ruby and emerald, amber and sapphire. Systems purred in response to his manipulations, seeking communion with the other vessels of the war flotilla, even through the warp's tides. Signals arrays reached out across the immaterial madness between his vessel and those of his peers, dancing between the ships bound for the Sol System. One by one the warriors of the III began to manifest, delicate patterns of hololithic light riven through with the contradictory static of the warp's malign tides.

'Ah, Eidolon,' the image of Julius Kaesoron hissed with curdled mirth. *'The closer we draw to the Throneworld, the more insufferable you become.'* It shuddered with laughter and the warped visage of the First Captain loomed forward. *'Still playing at lordship! The Phoenician has returned to us and the Legion is gathered. What do you gain by trying to rest your hand at the tiller?'*

'Someone has to make sure you don't plunge your vessels into a star on a whim, Julius,' Eidolon gurgled back. 'Let us not forget that I outrank you. Herding you and yours falls to me because I have earned my place. I have been trusted by our errant father.' He paused, hunching forward so that he was eye to eye with the rendition of the Favoured Son. 'Who was the first to join him at Ullanor?' he scoffed.

'You were quick to come to heel, true enough. Others had sought him while you dallied elsewhere. Hunting the Scars in futility, wasn't it? Before you bowed and scraped for Mortarion.' Kaesoron tittered and the image shook, light twisting around his ruined features. *'With such diverse interests, it's a wonder you ever came this far. I imagined that you and the forces you commanded would have idled, waiting, lost to your own desires rather than the masters we serve. Our new gods, the primarch, and the Warmaster.'*

'It is only fair that you see your own flaws and failings reflected in me, Julius,' Eidolon said. He shook his head and his lank hair fluttered gently, all lustre robbed by his rebirth. 'I have been fighting the Warmaster's battles. I sought to cage our enemies and break them. I remember what it means to serve the cause.'

'*Always on your own terms.*'

'There can be no other terms but mine.' Eidolon gestured, not to the hololith but past it.

Three kneeling figures moved in a single motion at his encouragement, rising to their feet and regarding their master with a mixture of emotions. Envy warred with respect. Fear was choked down by the pretence of pride. It bled from them in a potent mix, mirrored in every movement they made, in their stances, in the subtle purring of their armour.

Captain Malakris wore his ruination like a cloak of glory. He had scoured his armour clean of the purple and gold of the Emperor's Children and replaced it with a wild array of colours. Some of the shades that glistened upon his plate had no human name, having been culled from the warp itself. He had anointed himself with the blood of daemons – taken in combat or given willingly in esoteric pacts and unholy oaths – till he seemed to glow with the immaterium's fickle light. Tiny rows of needle teeth had begun to push themselves from the edges of his pauldrons, undoubtedly terminating as bony barbs within the armour itself, to scrape and cut at Malakris' flesh with every movement. His gauntlets were a set of matched lightning claws, once artfully rendered, now hooked like the talons of some exaggerated raptor. His helmet, long since brazenly fashioned into the screaming rictus of a bird of prey, was mag-locked at his hip, revealing his remade face.

The once rakish features of the warrior had been twisted like melting wax. Jewelled studs were driven bone-deep into his skull, and rings adorned the folds and flaps of warped and distended skin. In places along the scalp, it seemed that Malakris had intentionally flayed his skin and muscle away, and ivory glistened wetly in the harsh lights of the bridge.

By contrast Vocipheron maintained the lean, even elegant, lines of a blademaster of the III Legion. His armour had come through the early battles of the war with little desecration, save where the wounds had been patched with gold. The filled cracks sprawled like lustrous rivers across the perfect purple of his battle plate. Twin sabres were belted at his hips, their edges finely polished and the metal expertly maintained. They had been forged by Vocipheron's own hands, to the fascination and delight of the Legion's Techmarines. He wore his helmet, hiding the consummate warrior's sharp features and golden hair. Where Malakris was ruin and flux given form, Vocipheron held firm against the tides of excessive alteration. That he endured amidst such a brotherhood, a true paragon of the old Palatine Blades now cast into a pit of warrior-sybarites, spoke of his dedication and his self-control.

Eidolon almost envied him his surety.

Last of all was Til Plegua of the Kakophoni. The Ruin-singer was the zenith, the culmination, singularly everything that Malakris aspired to and Vocipheron reviled. His eyes had been pinned open, sutures biting into the flesh of one side of his face and the bone of the other. Til Plegua had, at the whim of the gods and through the transformative delight of the *Maraviglia*, flensed away the meat from the right side of his face, leaving a morbid rictus of grinning bone and perpetually tormented nerve-mesh, scrimshawed with strange symbols and intricate scenes of debauchery.

His armour was festooned with sonic amplifiers and vox-emitters, bolted and welded into the distended fabric of the plate. A myriad of insane colours swam between the mechanisms, so that he seemed more a madman's painting come to life than a warrior of the Emperor's Children. His throat pulsed and thrummed in mimicry of Eidolon's own sonic gifts, and the Lord Commander Primus knew that to hear Til speak was to court madness. Transcendent melodies still swam in his speech, his every utterance little more than a reflection of some vaster and more glorious work.

'My champions stand ready for the task,' Eidolon said simply, gesturing again, down past Kaesoron's smirking horror. 'I have taken the warriors of the Third Millennial as my own, and they have proven themselves to be admirable servants and fine company.' He hesitated, forcing a grin onto his twisted features. 'For the most part.'

'You never were a great judge of character, were you?' Kaesoron snorted as he spoke, and the hololith shimmered and sparked again. Between the flickers of projected light, something dwelt. Eidolon saw it in fractured moments, caught like an insect in amber, leering back at him with features that gave even him pause.

Daemon.

The thought rippled across his mind. He was no longer listening to Kaesoron's jibes and vainglorious boasts. There was only the presence which lurked behind and beyond his words. Fangs glistened wetly, set in a face wracked by delirious pleasure-pain. For a fleeting moment, Eidolon thought he saw an echo of the Phoenician in the thing's mania, but it was gone a second later. It held no true form. The liminal stuff of its being flowed before writhing in limitless mockery.

Brother…

The voice whispered into Eidolon's skull. Pain throbbed dully through his cranium, and he leant back, letting the flesh catch on the bone spurs of his throne. He thudded his skull against the metal and breathed out.

Kindred…

The thing whispered again, its every word dancing with revelation and promise. Eidolon knew that if he lowered his guard but a little then the presence would find purchase, slither in, hollow him out.

Daemons were nothing but dust and dreams, poisoned promises.

'*Brother?*' Kaesoron's voice had returned now. The First Captain spared Eidolon a withering look before he chuckled bleakly. '*You do not look well, Lord Commander Primus. Perhaps you should let your tame physicians tend to your maladies, eh?*' The image shuddered once more and Kaesoron looked away, turning his maddened gaze to the side and nodding. '*When next we speak, it shall be as we return home, guided by our father's hand. Then the feast can begin in earnest. I hope to see you upon the field, lord commander. It would be… truly exquisite to fight with you once again.*'

Eidolon merely nodded, teeth gritted. 'As I'm sure it would be to fight at your side, *Favoured Son.*' He forced his grimace to become a grin. 'Terra shall be the crucible and the culmination. There we shall be as we were always intended to be.'

Eidolon's mind roiled with the potential of what was to come. Terra itself, the Throneworld laid bare and yearning to their attentions. A populace to be made sport of and old rivals to be cast down. After Terra there would be time to build, for Fabius to experiment, for the Legion to truly blossom, and for his own ascent to become complete. He was the Lord Commander Primus. There would be a place for him in the new Imperium… Yet first that final barricade had to be surmounted.

The Palace had to be claimed and made ready, just as the thrones of the gods waited beyond the veil.

'*Soon all other enmities shall be set aside,*' Kaesoron intoned. The hololith flickered again and the ship shuddered as though in baleful sympathy. '*The time comes when you must at last–*'

'*Join us,*' the daemon breathed in place of the First Captain. It looked at Eidolon with milky eyes, cataracted and yet bright with immaterial fire. In that perfect moment, suspended before the dying image of Julius Kaesoron, it raised one clawed hand as though conducting a symphony, toying with the air to the tune of music only it could hear.

Then the ship was shaking and screaming, and all was reduced to fire and the laughter of those who dwelt beyond.

TWO

THE VEIL RENDS

Sirens flared through the madness of the bridge, high and shrill, long since augmented to seize the attention of a crew ruined by madness and overindulgence.

Eidolon was already in motion, surging up from his throne, bellowing orders at cringing slaves and unprepared warriors alike.

'Up, you mongrels!' he spat. 'To your stations! Give me clarity or I will have your skins.' Serfs spun and danced out of his way as he hurled himself towards the wailing consoles. Malakris was quicker, hand up and flashing, eyes alight with mirth. He brought a shining gauntlet round, smashing it into the side of a slave's skull. No sooner had the unfortunate fallen than he was upon him. Torturers' blades, plucked from his belt, glimmered in the faltering light as he began to cut and stab, prying free skin in long strips. Blood joined the paint upon his armour, and he leant forward, licking the screaming man's life from the blade with savage glee.

Witch light burned in the high vaults of the ceiling, illuminating gaudy murals that leered down with too-real eyes. The ship breathed, the walls pressing in, bowing outwards with some strange internal force. Malakris looked up, fascinated, enraptured by the yearning things that waited beyond.

Vocipheron held. He stood, ramrod straight, hand upon his blade, waiting for the storm to break around him. Til Plegua followed in Eidolon's wake, his sonic weaponry humming, building to an inevitable crescendo.

Shutters rose with a sudden clatter, rattling back up and into their housings, exposing the roiling madness of the warp. The immaterium clawed at the ship with spiteful longing. The struggling Geller field rippled and fluctuated as hungry faces stretched across its skin of tenuous reality. The vox crackled to life, filling the already cacophonous space with fresh screaming. The Navigator's link was alive with pain, broadcasting the man's agony into the open air. Malakris cooed as he heard it, head snapping back like a dog scenting meat, addicted to the spice of suffering.

Eidolon turned from the addled lunatic and fixed his gaze upon Vocipheron. 'See to the Navigator. We will break from the warp and then see what can be salvaged from the wretched bastard.' He spat upon the decking. 'I want to know where we are. We need to restore communications with the rest of the fleet. We stand upon the brink of the greatest battle, and I refuse to be seen as a laggard.'

Vocipheron nodded and turned away, pushing through the crew and out of sight.

The Lord Commander Primus watched him leave and then turned back to the crew. He had scooped up *Glory Aeterna*, and hefted the hammer in a sweeping gesture, pointing it at the tormented void beyond. 'I want us out of this miasma – the sooner the better. If I am not indulged presently then I shall begin breaking bones.'

A chorus of assents rose from the slave pits and station alcoves that surrounded him. Eidolon stalked between them, Til and Malakris at his heels, peering down at the desperate and the mutilated.

The frisson of panic that had saturated the bridge was laced with the stink of human excretion as they toiled beneath their master's gaze. Every now and then Eidolon would lower the hammer's unpowered edge to the nape of a slave's neck, watching them tense. Sweat ran freely down their scarred skin; tongues lapped at lips with fretful longing. Torn between the desire for death and the hope of yet more wretched life, they both yearned for the attention of the legionaries and hungered for the culmination of the warriors' wrath.

'Most noble lord,' one of the slaves mewled, 'we are sensor-blind and warp-locked. We cannot break from the immaterium. We have tried, yet we seem suspended in the storm. It holds us on both sides of the veil, caught in the claw of the gods.'

'I do not want excuses,' Eidolon hissed. 'I want–'

To be free.

The voice breathed into his ear, rippling with laughter. Eidolon spun, weapon up and ignited in a heartbeat. His face twisted into a snarl as he confronted… nothing. Malakris looked at him askance, leering at the Lord Commander Primus as he scented weakness.

'You seem skittish, Eidolon,' he purred. 'Hardly becoming of a lord commander.'

'If you think you can do better, captain, then I invite you to try. It would lift my spirits to watch you flail vaingloriously at the open air, expecting that others will follow your commands.' Eidolon sneered and brought the hammer up to Malakris' shoulder. 'Remember your place, whelp.'

'How could I forget?' Malakris whispered, leaning nearer to the weapon's embrace. His flesh drew dangerously close to the active power field. Static discharge snapped like lightning between the armoured plate of the warrior and the glimmering weapon, earthing through Malakris' bones and making the studs and rings embedded in his flesh sing. 'Is it only the Phoenician, I wonder, who can knock you from your pedestal?'

'Your speculation bores me, Malakris. I suggest you find yourself another hobby,' Eidolon said, his slack mouth stirring into a smirk as he leant closer. 'I am not so easily replaced. You, though? I could carve a hundred bastards from the flesh of the Third and any of them would be your match.'

Before the other warrior could reply, the hydraulic hiss of an opening door drew both their attentions.

Vocipheron strode back into the chamber, features set hard. One arm was swept out to shield a hunched figure in tattered robes. Golden chains, broken now, hung limply from the figure's wrists and ankles, trailing behind them as they staggered onto the bridge.

The blademaster stopped and nudged the man forwards. The hood of the robes slipped back and Eidolon beheld the ruin that had become of Navigator Primary Toshen Melar.

He had clawed at his face, nails digging so deeply into the flesh that bloody furrows were carved down his cheeks. His mortal eyes were gone, gouged out with his own fingers, but it was the horror of his forehead that captivated Eidolon's gaze. The Navigator had removed his bindings and torn the warp eye from his skull. The Lord Commander Primus let his gaze move down the bloodied robes to the hands that Toshen held out, trembling, to the gory detritus smeared there, still aglow with some inner light.

It was a powerful thing for a Navigator to pluck out his gift.

'It sings,' Toshen whispered. He raised his empty sockets as though still capable of seeing, fixing them impossibly upon Eidolon. 'A kingly voice calls and sings, the sea beyond keens back in kind, and we all tumble down into the abyss with them. Better darkness than that. I have made my choice. I have been chosen…'

'Restrain him,' Eidolon said, and stepped forward. 'Why must we always be stymied by the folly of lesser men?' No one answered. He shook his head and hefted *Glory Aeterna* high.

He had never liked Navigators. Not truly. There were few who actively courted their presence and fewer still of their breed who were worthy of attention. A stunted nobility, cultivated out of necessity. Each of the houses was a scheming nest of mutation, its scions' humanity long since sieved away and transmuted by the rigours of some past Dark Age.

Tools at best, he thought as he looked upon Toshen's mutilation. *Broken ones, now.*

'It sees you,' Toshen burbled suddenly, raising one hand to point a quaking finger at Eidolon. 'It knows you. There is no succour here. Only the inevitable end. Only–'

The hammer fell.

The crackling head of the weapon atomised Toshen's skull and the man's body tumbled back, trailing his golden chains and a dusting of burnt blood. His hands flailed at the empty air and the dull remnants of his warp eye spattered upon the decking. Vocipheron flinched backwards, shocked by his master's sudden wrath, as Eidolon stalked forward, glaring down at the corpse.

'This is the price of weakness! Do you hear me? Each of you owes me service, fealty, and I expect you to deliver it. Any who falter shall die, by my hand, long before you reach the hands of our enemies!' He whirled about, face contorted with rage. Veins twitched in his throat, the flesh rippling with the barely contained scream already building there. 'Break us from this cage, or I will shatter every last one of you in turn.'

He turned and left the bridge, leaving only mewling slaves and useless servants in his wake. Still, now eternally at his ear, came the mockery.

THREE

HAUNTED

Are we jumping at spectres now? Driven mad by the shadow of fear?

Eidolon scowled as he moved through the raucous corridors of the *Wage of Sin*. He passed through places where all lights had been doused to better obscure whatever deviancies flourished in the darkness, into other chambers where every lumen had been overloaded to furious intensity. In some, they flickered and pulsed with new colours while sirens screamed on and on forever.

Exploration was no longer the domain of the shipmasters and scouts of the Great Crusade, nor was experimentation the sole purview of the ever-expanding Apothecarion of the Legion. It had been incised upon the heart of every warrior of the III. They had become the true embodiments of the Emperor's dead vision, reshaping its corpse into something worthy of the galaxy's true masters.

The gods.

Eidolon chuckled at the thought. The gods of old had risen

up, as he had, to claim the galaxy that was promised to them. Fulgrim was a part of them now, dancing to the tune of dread Slaanesh, and Lupercal – for all his failings and flaws, for all his bastard Cthonian savagery – was ripe with their power. Eidolon knew there were many amongst the Legions who had pledged to the Warmaster who would say that it had simply reverted to its natural state, that Chaos was as intrinsic to life as breathing, yet he knew them for liars.

Everything was different now, past the veil of life and death. He had returned from beyond that threshold, remade and reborn, as surely as Fulgrim had vaulted forth into eternity.

Eidolon had become the Soul-Severed. A broken thing, made exemplar in his destitution. He had nothing and no one left to fear.

Yet still the creeping malice coiled about him, even here in his fastness. The warp clamoured, hungry and urgent, whispering through the bones of the ship like the caress of a lover. The siren song recurred about them, teasing talons down the spine of every warrior therein, seeking purchase. Perhaps it had been with them since Isstvan and the glorious atrocities there. Or maybe it had come later, when his eyes had truly been opened.

'The men are unruly, lord,' came a voice from behind him. Eidolon did not slow or cease. He knew Til Plegua's broken speech well enough. 'Especially Malakris' coterie. They may play the tame pack, but deprive them of their meat and they shall turn. Whatever haunts our steps has them in upheaval.'

'They are of the Third Legion,' Eidolon said. 'They are ever unruly in these nights.'

'You should discipline them,' Plegua slurred. 'If you would rule as the Phoenician rules, then they should be shown the error of their ways.'

'As I was? Is that it?'

'Of course not, lord,' Plegua laughed. His caustic joy stained the air and the walls trembled. Gilding shook free from the faded murals and broken statuary that lined the corridor.

'Taking their heads though… that does hold a certain appeal.' Eidolon joined the Kakophoni warrior in his mirth. 'Perhaps I would mount them upon my throne, or present them to Fulgrim when we gain orbit around Terra, eh? More dead sons for our beloved father. He is *ever so fond of them.*'

He could hear it again. Laughter behind their joy, scraping at the edges of his awareness like a whetstone against a blade. The shadows darkened, lengthened, till it seemed there were cold talons within – reaching for him with avarice.

Eidolon. Lord commander. Brother…

Things moved there, in the darkness, at once eternal and Neverborn, and the ship shuddered with their hunger. Spasms of unreality moved through the great ship's bones, aftershocks of the warp's cloying fury.

'There are some who say we are cursed,' Eidolon ventured conversationally, ignoring the signs and omens. 'At least, to a greater degree than we previously found ourselves.'

'Mortals, no doubt,' Plegua trilled. 'Their fear sullies the ship, left like spoor.'

'Yet perhaps they're right,' the Lord Commander Primus allowed. 'The warp speaks in a thousand voices, each one true and yet forked against us. We are trapped. Not our fellows. Not the Legion. Us. It is we who are here now, caught in the viper's jaws.'

'How do we break free of it?' Plegua's throat spasmed. Every part of him twitched and moved, hungry for conflict, to exalt once again in the song that drove him.

'We find the source of the warp contagion and we drive it out, be that by brute force or what passes for sorcery amongst our ilk.' He paused for a moment, catching a glimpse of his sneering reflection in the metal of a nearby bulkhead. It mocked him, eyes lambent and fixed upon him, before it skittered away into the darkness of the world beyond. He scowled again.

'We have no true sorcerers, lord,' Til enunciated carefully. 'We are exalted. Not polluted.'

'The gods provide, my friend, even against their own schemes. Look at what we have made of ourselves by simply seizing hold of our biology,' Eidolon purred. 'Let our brothers scrabble for position as they wish. It is I who will forge our path to freedom, carved from flesh and blood such that even Fabius would recoil from it. We shall stand at the Phoenician's side when the final days dawn upon Terra. Go to your men, stir them to the task. I want to know what the warp's song speaks. I will seek guidance elsewhere. Then, together, we shall undo the knots that bind us. Terra waits, and I shall be the implement that delivers us there.'

As the Legion had changed, so had the Apothecarion.

The III had always possessed a larger body of Apothecaries than other Legions, a consequence of their early struggles. Those who had emerged from the tumult of the Blight, trained under the watchful eye of the Spider, had become prodigies. Few Astartesian gene-crafters had risen to challenge the Master of Mankind, but those of the Emperor's Children had succeeded in improving upon the work of the great creator. Fabius had scattered the seeds of that knowledge to the wind and watched as they bore strange fruit across the galaxy.

What has it bought us? The thought coiled treacherously within Eidolon's mind as he advanced into the once cold confines of the Apothecarion. He had dismissed Plegua to rouse the Kakophoni in force, to see if their intrinsic understanding of the warp could aid them. The walk from the bridge to the frigid domain of Von Kalda had been marred only by the persistent tremor in the ship.

He ignored it now, just as he did not acknowledge the experimental horrors that writhed within their glass jars, imprisoned for nothing less than Von Kalda's predatory curiosity.

Once, he had languished beneath Fabius' knife in an oubliette much like this one. An abattoir of the old ideals. This was a less elegant space, its ribbed ceiling bearing spatters of blood and flesh from the tables below. The scent of vitae and preservatives filled the chamber, rendering it close and septic.

We have become as we were always meant to be, he thought again. *Remade and reborn. So much sacrificed to the fire so we might rise triumphant. This may be Fabius' design, but it is the Legion's becoming.*

Von Kalda was already present, puttering over something at one of the *Wage of Sin*'s many anatomical benches. The warrior's armour was pale white, pearlescent under the harsh lights of the Apothecarion, stained red to the elbow with spilled blood, mottled through with stranger fluids. He turned, helmless, his oddly childlike face creasing momentarily with confusion, before he returned to his work.

'It has been some time since you have bothered me in my... official capacity, lord. To what do I owe the pleasure?'

'We are under attack,' Eidolon stated plainly. He pushed forward and loomed over the Apothecary. Despite their shared heritage, Eidolon was the more massive presence, dominating the Apothecarion as easily as he did the battlefield.

His eyes twitched left and right as he took in the ghoulish tableau that sprawled around the space. A serf had been vivisected, pinned out in the manner of a surgical specimen, his organs littered around his body cavity like a profusion of discarded crimson fruit.

Von Kalda wiped his bloody hands against the thighs of his plate before clapping them together. 'Aren't we always?' He turned away from the Lord Commander Primus and reached for a scalpel, lifted it and examined the edge. 'The ship's transit has been arrested, hasn't it? I heard the sirens… But if this were Sol then I imagine there would be a degree more urgency in deploying. Where are we?'

Eidolon hesitated. Even here, alone but for the two of them, he could feel eyes at his back and foetid breath coiling at his neck. 'We are all haunted, equerry,' he said. Von Kalda had served Eidolon ably these years, in his capacity as his equerry and representative. A stalwart and trusted soul, dependable as Eidolon had wrested control of a third of the Legion and set himself after the Khan. 'Whatever haunts us has played its hand at last. There are no longer merely whispers at our backs, but a blade. That is why I require you.'

Von Kalda tutted. He replaced the scalpel and lifted his still-bloody fingers to lap at the clinging vitae. His tongue flickered over the digits and then retracted, circling his too-fine lips. 'Require my services? And yet you seem the picture of health,' he mused. 'Insofar as you can be judged. Better than this.' He gestured to the corpse. 'I was curious as to what was killing him, but accelerating the process has only left me bored.'

'We have no time for your damned distractions!' Eidolon snapped. 'I will not be denied my place at the table. Terra lies before us! Terra! The very heart of the war, slipping from my grasp. Do you think our father will look kindly on those who tarried? I will *not* suffer his indignities again. Never again.'

Von Kalda swept his arm around and the carcass slid from the bench with a wet, meaty slap. 'You will not be forgotten, lord.' He stopped and carefully considered his next words, sensing his master's choler. 'You are the Lord Commander Primus. I serve at your whim.'

Eidolon looked away, as though ashamed. 'There is something more here. I feel it in the pits of my soul. Something hungry. Waiting for some sign of weakness so that it might pounce. Claim me like a piece upon a board.'

'I am no psyker, lord.' Von Kalda scratched absently at his chin. 'If something ails your song-touched soul, could you not employ the Kakophoni? They know the warp's sweet melody well enough.'

'Songs lie. They mislead as easily as dreams,' Eidolon said. His gaze had taken on a distant tinge, yet his eyes were brighter than they had been, irises gleaming through the murk with a suddenly predatory iridescence. 'I require clarity. To know that my senses are my own and that some daemon has not crawled into my soul.'

Von Kalda raised the narthecium gauntlet, letting the blades and drills catch in the harsh light. He watched as needles extended, tasting the air as readily as they would soon bite flesh.

'My studies have encompassed the physical and the supernal,' he replied. He leant forward and drove the needle in at Eidolon's neck. Air hissed from the wound alongside a sluggish trickle of glistening blood. The Lord Commander Primus tensed as he felt the prong move through skin and flesh to bury itself into bone. 'There are no true metrics for such things, not yet, but it is an evolving field.' He paused, watching the clicking calibrations of his narthecium. 'Perhaps some sort of treatment that could safeguard you against such things...'

Eidolon's eyes darted suddenly, away from the violation, his neck fixed and unable to move. Laughter drifted on the recycled yet still musky air. He followed its path. Every reflective surface was suddenly dull, opaque, save for his gurning reflection.

Eidolon...

The voice whispered, a hiss at the limits of his perception. The reflections began to shift and change, flowing like hot wax. One of them caught fire, throwing its head back in a suddenly screaming rictus. The flesh sloughed from another's skull, leaving only the grinning death's head, sinews tight and clinging.

Eyes burst. Tongues caught in throats, giving the image a

weakling death as it choked and fell to its knees. Eidolon looked on impassively, his mouth only flickering into a smirk in response.

'Is this all you have for me?' he said. 'I do not fear what I have already conquered.'

'Lord?' Von Kalda had turned as he withdrew the needle, eyes suddenly fixed upon him, painted with old fear that sat ill in his too-young flesh.

Eidolon blinked and the reflections disappeared. He was simply himself once again.

'Just the architect of our miseries toying with me,' Eidolon snarled. 'The daemons that haunt us think me weak, to be cowed by dilute signs and shallow wonders.' He turned from the table with a laugh and strode towards the door, readying himself to venture back into the unwelcoming hell the vessel was becoming. 'If you cannot be of use to me, Apothecary, then I shall carve this problem out myself. There is no time for experiments or exploratory treatments. The enemy is upon us now. We are stranded. I shall summon Malakris and Vocipheron. Plegua as well.'

Eidolon raised one gauntleted hand and clenched it into a fist, taunting fate itself to strike him down.

'Soon enough we will cut to the heart of this.'

They met in a loose gathering of not-quite-equals, upon one of the great vessel's primary armament decks.

Eidolon stood at the centre, flanked by Plegua and his other Kakophoni. A hooting chorus surrounded them, rising to fill the vast vaulted chamber to the increasing irritation of the other factions. Malakris' brood of killers were growing ever more diverse in their mutilation, a creeping monstrosity that had danced across their armour and flesh.

Malakris raised his hands, the lightning claws that smouldered there more at home amidst the murder-pits of the VIII than the warrior conclaves of the III. But then, Eidolon mused, he had always been a brutal creature, even before the Dark Prince had warped his bellicose soul into a thing of barbed edges and shattered mirrors.

Vocipheron's coterie kept their distance from Malakris' motley band, hands locked upon the hilts of their blades as though some internecine squabble was inevitable.

'Peace, brothers,' Eidolon said, and his words rippled out from him in a wave. All but the Kakophoni winced away from his display, the power that radiated with his every utterance. The sacs at his throat swelled and trilled behind his words. All present knew what the Lord Commander Primus was capable of. They had watched his scream shatter his foes, reducing them to little more than broken and bloody smears before him.

'We are called like dogs and expected not to raise our voices?' Malakris barked. 'I will not tarry like one of his callow blade-masters.' He gestured dismissively towards Vocipheron. 'We should be free of this nightmare. Out and into the galaxy, burning towards Terra!' His claws sparked as he stalked forwards, not yet raising them in challenge.

'Spare me,' Eidolon snapped, rounding on Malakris with *Glory Aeterna* suddenly up and ignited. 'You would drown us in your wretched pursuits. We would not come to Terra whole, nor at all. I command here. The Third Millennial is mine, by right of rank.' He turned and regarded Vocipheron with cold judgement. 'What of you? Do you have some insight as to how we should proceed?'

'You are the Lord Commander Primus,' the swordsman said. 'Your will guides us. That is enough for me.'

'Coward,' Malakris called, rich with mockery. 'You worry about what squats in my soul, but at least there is something there in me. You have hollowed yourself out, made yourself weak, all because you cling to your skill like a drowning man to debris.'

'Enough!' Eidolon boomed suddenly. The walls shook and bowed in, plates bent and ruptured by his fury. Both warriors staggered back. Their fellows, almost as one, went to their knees. The Kakophoni keened, flesh rippling with joyous rapture.

He could hear them speak, their low whispers at odds with their normal vocal fury, echoed by something else. Something waiting just beyond reality's skin.

The song. *The song.* **The song!**

There had always been the warp's melody, skirling and blaring with all of Kynska's borrowed grandeur and twisted skill. Yet now something else sounded through it and behind it, building up from whisper to crescendo. A call to arms. A summons home. He had thought it Fulgrim's siren song, but it was different, more nuanced. A bespoke melody shaped for Eidolon's tortured form and splintered soul.

'You are gathered here,' Eidolon went on, 'because you are my commanders. My chosen warriors. The elect amongst our multitudes. Of all those who strive for our varied perfections, you have risen to be paragons. Warriors of the Third. My warriors.' He smiled his broken smile. 'We are needed at Terra. I will not be stranded in the immaterium while the final battle is decided. None of us shall. Upon the Throneworld's soil there are wonders yet to be born. We shall match our might against the best of the Emperor's slaves and grind them into the dust.'

As though in sympathetic response, the ship shook again. Beyond their hull the Geller field was being battered, recoiling from the potency of the warp's fury. Another blaring siren began to sound, lending its music to the bleak symphonies of the III.

They would die if there was not action. Decisive action.

'It shall be so,' Vocipheron said. The swordsman stepped forward, his sense of duty braving Eidolon's wrath.

'Of course!' Eidolon said. He lowered the hammer and placed one gnarled hand upon Vocipheron's shoulder. 'We spent too long baiting and hunting the Khan and his mongrels as they fled towards Terra. All that wasted effort ensures that I am owed my pound of flesh. I wish to cross swords with the Praetorian and carve him apart like his pretty little walls. I want to break the Great Angel's wings beneath my boots and taste the marrow from his hollow bones. These and more are my dreams.'

Dreams, the voice purred again, and Eidolon remembered…

Armoured fingers lifting his chin to gaze upon perfection. A smile as blinding as the sun upon the white marble of the square. A face wrought with absolute genetic mastery, looking down upon him with love. 'Rise, lord commander,' the Phoenician whispered.

He shook away the unbidden memory with a scowl. 'There is an ache within my soul, a call that we cannot ignore. We will hunt down whatever warp-born thing has us in its talons, and we shall break its grip, finger by finger.'

Malakris leant forward avariciously. A line of acid drool had begun to dribble from one corner of his mouth. 'Ah, to fight the Neverborn again. They love and despise me so. Offering their blessings and their curses, their lust and their revulsion.' He brushed a hand down the blood-anointed plate of his armour. 'It will be a joy to court that once more.'

'Disgusting,' Vocipheron said, and shook his head. 'Lord Commander Primus, I cannot understand why you allow this parasite to continue to draw breath and sow his treachery. You should let me end him.'

'Perhaps one day,' Eidolon mused. 'But not today. Today I have need of you both. My rough-edged blade and my flawless implement.'

Behind them a door opened with a sigh of releasing pressure. Eidolon turned with a smile and bowed his head.

'Finally. The last of us arrives.'

Von Kalda stood, his despoiled narthecium still dripping with mortal gore. He looked at Eidolon, nodding with simple respect, before falling in at his master's side. The others observed him, reactions flickering from grudging respect to outright disdain.

Eidolon ignored them all, focused now upon his task. Upon the hunt.

'Shall we begin?'

FOUR

———————————

BENEATH THE SKIN

They delved into the depths of the great ship, their force like a sharpened blade plunged towards the heart.

Eidolon led from the front, as was his right and his duty, navigating by instinct alone. Pain sang in his skull, flaring bright and then ebbing away as he followed the ineffable path prepared for him. Every creak of his bones and sudden nerve spasm was an indicator, a soul-deep ache pulling at him, till the steps felt as though they were no longer his own. A powerlessness that he despised and yet was compelled to obey.

Behind him came Malakris and Vocipheron, while Plegua and one of his loyal Kakophoni brought up the rear. The other warrior was called Darven, his lean face framed by vast sonic amplification engines, drowning him in the mechanisms of his own secret song. His gaze remained fixed ahead, his eyes pinned open and his jaw held wide by steel bars.

Bring me your finest, Eidolon had told Plegua. *I need my faithful at my back.*

Von Kalda toyed with his narthecium, processing the read-
ings he had taken from Eidolon. In the interests of pursuing
his avenues of research he had practically volunteered for the
duty, even though his capacity as equerry bade him to attend
his master. He was no coward; his motivations were merely
evolving – becoming more esoteric and self-serving.

The corridors of the *Wage of Sin* had once been dependable,
labyrinthine as any voidship yet understandable by transhuman
minds. Now they had grown strange, twisted by the corrosive
touch of the warp. Doorways no longer reliably led where they
should. Lights danced in the corridors in strange configurations,
drifting from their lumen-mounts to wander like corpse fires,
luring in the unwary. Minor deviances, more annoyances than
any true mockery. Eidolon did not doubt that these changes
would only grow more intense as the hunt continued.

Pillars heaved upwards, bracing the distant ceilings. Each
one was no longer purely metal but had slowly transmuted
into living bone in places, threaded with questing capillaries.
Eidolon reached out with one hand and brushed his fingertips along the living canvas, watching as the vessels contracted
at his touch.

'Fascinating what the immaterial is capable of,' he breathed. 'All
things are remade by the Dark Prince's attentions.' Eidolon raised
Glory Aeterna and let the power field cascade over the ivory surface. He could hear the pained screams of something, infrasonic,
scouring at his awareness, scintillating his very soul. 'But this is
my ship,' he concluded, 'and the only hand that shapes it is mine.'

The ship seemed to recoil at his words. Weapons were raised
and the warriors fanned out around Eidolon as his speech
echoed about the vastness of the space.

Mine…

Things moved in the shadows above them, made of liquid
blackness that crawled and skittered along the ceiling. The

clattering of their claws as they attained physicality sent rains of tiny sparks down over the gathered warriors. Lithe muscles contracted in the darkness, pushing them onwards, trailing tanned human leather and spikes of black metal. They looked down upon Eidolon with suddenly corporeal eyes, burning pinpricks set in the black sclerae of an oceanic predator.

'Ours,' they purred as they moved, sliding and gliding down from the heights like descending angels. Wrought from horror and wonder, every mortal dream and deviance given form. The handmaidens of the Dark Prince pivoted off the walls and landed around the knot of warriors in a loose circle. Six of them stood before the Lord Commander Primus. The lead one, crowned in human bone and soft meat, bowed low before him, a crustacean's claw scraping against the decking. The sound made Eidolon's ears ache, a resonance so potent he felt it in his soul.

'You are known to us. Soul sworn and pacted. You belong to the Prince Who Waits, the Thirsting Queen, They Who Are Divine. God-promised souls, eaters of the old enemy, destroyers of the new foe. The Anathema's by-blows, returned to us.'

'We are not yours,' Eidolon said, and laughed. 'You are merely the dregs of the Dark Prince. You who promise everything and are yet nothing.'

The Neverborn's face creased with amusement and the sound it made was like the tinkling of tiny bells. Greater peals rang out behind them, with the rumble of distant thunder. Eidolon was aware, intimately, of the creature's transitory nature. It was a fleeting thing. Ephemeral and unknowable, an echo of a greater godhead. He watched as it laughed and as its face flowed from one visage to another.

Here it was a bright young warrior, a youth in his prime, ready to raise spear and sword for his distant master. A flicker and it was instead a nubile woman, her features speaking of a lifetime of pain and pleasure. A moment more and it wore the painted face of a beautiful corpse, terrible and yet alluring in its androgyny.

'You could stand as a king in the sight of the gods and yet you preen at the foot of your father,' the daemon-thing cajoled. *'You could be so much more than you are. What is Terra when there are worlds yet unconquered? Do you not remember what it was to stand as a true master of war, instead of merely a demigod's bastard?'* It raised its claws, cutting at the air. *'I could show you, little princeling. I could show you the notes of the song you grasp for. I, Liadress, the Singing Blade That Cuts With Each Caress, could help you follow in your father's footsteps. You need not grovel, when the Eternal Chorus could sound across all–'*

Eidolon swung the hammer, the weapon spitting fitful lightning as he heaved forwards against Liadress. The daemon slid backwards, so fast it was a mere blur and a hiss of motion. Its sisters moved to replace it, a line of five chittering and cooing monsters. Beautiful monsters, hideously delectable ruins of the mortal form, warped and twisted beyond human conception.

Their claws flashed out, leaving bright contrails through the air as they sought purchase against arms and armour. Eidolon watched the power field flare and spark as the first strikes were turned aside. His own men were already moving, forming a protective cordon, stepping forwards to aid their master. Von Kalda stepped back, raising his pistol to fire.

'There need not be discord between us, princeling. Not when the Shattered King has such sights for you. Have you seen him in the mirrors of your soul? Does he yet whisper?'

Eidolon blinked away his surprise. He had thought whatever force pursued him was some figment of his father, yet now it had a name. The Shattered King. A petty and melodramatic title, redolent of the warp's excesses.

Eidolon gestured and his men answered the pronouncement with death and fury.

The Kakophoni committed their twinned weapons in great sweeping arcs of devastation. Even as the daemons dodged the sonic blasts, they tore through the cover. Pillars burst apart in clouds of iron and bone, stumps gouting ferrous blood into the air. The vast ceiling, distant and impossible, didn't sag as they tore the supports out from under it. The Neverborn capered and tittered as they weaved beneath falling masonry and the immense showers of gore. Eidolon pushed forwards through the debris, smashing vast fragments aside with *Glory Aeterna*.

'Broken little monster,' Liadress mocked. *'When we see your father, we shall sing the songs of your doom. We shall offer up the hymns of your delightful end. He shall know, Soul-Severed, that you begged like a dog at the end. Never to be consort or champion, but to die – unmourned amidst the ashes of your ambition.'*

'I will not die without setting foot upon Terra,' Eidolon hissed. He ducked the swipe of a claw and drove the hammer forward, narrowly missing the lithe daemon. Liadress hissed and pivoted back, before its ire dissolved into tinkling laughter. Eidolon's strike had disrupted the artful asymmetry of the dance, blunting the arc of its graceful assault. 'If the gods wish to stop me then they should send better than mongrels such as you.'

Liadress drove forward, screaming as it did. Blades of chitin and bone slammed against the head of the hammer, driving it down. He could smell burning flesh and the pungent musk exuding from every pore the thing possessed. He gritted his teeth and hefted the hammer up. Mortal and immortal strength clashed as everything burned and broke around them. Yet there was only the moment.

Eidolon had fought countless battles – commanding massed men and fighting alone. He had led warriors of the III Legion into war across a hundred battlefields, even before the betrayal had set them against their fellows. He had taken the time to guide cohorts of the Imperial Army, binding them to his Legion in webs of respect and admiration.

He braced as another rain of blows fell upon him, seeking to dislodge his grip upon the hammer's haft. He felt blood well between the plates of his armour, staggering back as the daemon's assault finally found his flesh. It raised the crimson-smeared claw to its lips and its long tongue gnarled about the chitin, lapping Eidolon's lifeblood.

'*Weak,*' the daemon burbled. '*Will you fight as meekly against the Anathema in his own Palace? Will you falter at the first hurdle? Buckle before the walls? Not a champion. Not chosen… simply chaff.*'

'Be silent!' Eidolon snarled. He felt his choler rise. His throat bulged and he reared back, letting the daemon's barbed claws clatter uselessly against the floor. Behind him he could hear his men fighting. He felt the surge of sonic force as Darven finally succumbed to the enemy, his weapon screaming before his voice and song were silenced forever.

Eidolon would not go gently. He would fight and rage against fate until the universe burned down around him. He was a lord commander, *the* Lord Commander Primus. No mere slave of the Dark Prince would shame him.

'*Death is sweet, yet service can be sweeter. The King waits! He waits and he hungers! You will be his, your warriors shall bend the knee! Serve and be spared. Resist and your skin shall be our leather. Your flesh our meat, your blood our wine!*'

His eyes flashed with raw amusement as he advanced upon Liadress. He kindled his fury, directed it, let it flood through him in a wave. Eidolon's jaw distended. The scream bubbled up through him, directed out through his modified throat, yet resonating through every pore. Every part of him was alive with it, filled with and fuelled by it.

The wall of sound drove Liadress back, screaming. It hurled the lesser daemons from their feet and cracked the stones beneath their bodies. Malakris and Vocipheron both staggered back, the blow rocking them but not overturning them. Von Kalda swayed, more used to his master's abilities, moving his body between Eidolon and the daemons. Only Plegua truly weathered the storm, unbowed by the display, invigorated by the power unleashed.

Eidolon sprang forward, hammer raised, even as the daemon spun back to meet him. He let it slip down, dropping the hammer to his side, feinting the blow. His fist, with all his rage behind it, clattered against its claws. Once, twice, three times. The chitin cracked. Liadress' eyes went wide with sudden surprise. Eidolon smiled.

He struck again and Liadress tumbled back, hissing with pain. 'Is this not part of your being?' he taunted. 'You exalt in inflicting it, and in bearing it. Why then is the agony I gift you not sweet?'

'Mongrel thing of flesh!' Liadress snarled. *'Do you think you are the better servant? That the Dark Prince loves you more than us?'*

He paused for a moment, luxuriating in the sounds of blades as they tore through flesh. Vocipheron and Malakris had rallied at last, bringing claw and sword to bear against the daemons. He let his eyes flicker to the plunging, lightning-rimed weapons as they cut and thrust. Plegua drove his boot into the chest of one and unleashed a murderous dirge, point-blank, from his great sonic weapon.

The daemon burst apart in a shower of immaterial viscera and glistening blood. One of its purple claws bounced away from the detonating body, still gouging at the floor as it struck the ground, over and over. Even in death the things fought, their very existence clinging to reality with a murderous tenacity that Eidolon could almost envy.

'You think yourself a prince of war, but you are nothing next to the Shattered King!'

'Show me this King, and we shall test the truth of it.' Eidolon sniffed. He turned *Glory Aeterna* over in his hands and stepped forward, raising it above his head. He brought the hammer down. The lightning-wreathed head of it tore through Liadress' distorted skull, atomising what passed for the thing's brain. Iridescent gore fountained into the air, spattering against Eidolon's warped pink armour, searing the plate into a spreading riot of non-colours where it landed. He let the hammer sink to his side and moderated his breathing. Eidolon's hearts hammered in his chest, pounding against his ribcage with the sudden rush of adrenaline.

To kill was his purpose. That had never changed, not since the earliest days upon Terra. As a warrior he had fought and slain individually, as a company commander he had learned what it meant to lead men – mortal and Astartes alike – yet it was only as a lord commander that he had truly understood and mastered that.

Eidolon had turned battle into an art long before Fabius' transformations had infected them, long before Laeran's salt caress had shaped them, body and soul, root and stem. He had fought and bled across the Emperor's expanding dominions, then followed their contractions as the Imperium sickened, shrinking back upon itself under the influence of its disloyal children.

Then, as now, the only way was forward.

Eidolon stalked past the gathered warriors and scowled as he turned, migraine pain flickering through his skull. Somewhere in the recesses of his soul, something was laughing, making his body tremble with a distant and shared joy. Convulsions wracked him as though his chest cavity were being shaken by applause, rattling his bones and making his hearts contract and falter. He could feel it now. The squatting monster, the pressure-presence that thrummed within his very being.

'Enough games,' he growled. 'We will find this Shattered King and break it so utterly that it will never dare to test me again.'

FIVE

THE SHATTERED KING

The ship shook around them, wracked by tides that only psykers could perceive.

The belly of the *Wage of Sin* had metastasised, taken by the touch of the warp to be shaped at the whim of the Shattered King. Stairways to nowhere extruded through decking; doors opened onto plain steel walls or stretched away into distant and rapturous infinities.

Its very presence was poison, worming through the veins of the ship, twisting it into something unnatural – even by the standards of the III Legion. Windows had appeared in some places, scenes of terrible beauty rendered in stained glass, every shard weeping with blood and tears.

All the reflections watched him – with his own clouded eyes, with his corpse-pallid face, with the visages of the long dead.

Eidolon. His name echoed in a longing refrain, whispered from countless lips. Catching upon his mind like chains.

The warp's madness stared at him, and he stared back. Not

for the first time, Eidolon wondered what it was like to see through warp-addled eyes. Perhaps when it was over, he would find some example of the witchbreed, drink down their memories and taste their gift.

His gauntleted hands twitched greedily.

Impulses, surging through his bloodstream, saturating his mind, let Eidolon know that he was still alive. Still able to act upon the game, to be a player upon the stage.

As your father taught you, he thought. *Now he preens, with Terra in his sights, roused from beyond the veil. Free to be a slave. To the gods. To Horus. To his own appetites.*

Eidolon hated Fulgrim and yet he still bore that fawning adoration that had so defined his existence. His hand had been the hand to wound him, the will to reshape him. That demanded some morsel of respect. Perhaps one day there would be an accord between them, if not a reckoning...

'Little sport,' Malakris grumbled as they continued onwards. The captain had taken to following close behind Von Kalda, reaching for him almost playfully with his kindled claws, letting them snap at the air. Drenched in their blood, anointed in their malice, Malakris still could not see that he was little different to the daemons they had fought. Eidolon might have pitied him once. Now, he was merely frustrated.

'The true challenge lies ahead,' Vocipheron put in. The swordsman shared Eidolon's agitation. His weapon swept through the air, cutting without target yet ripe with intent. 'These falsehoods are distractions, as all things of the warp are.'

'Pretty distractions,' Malakris cooed. 'Daemons taunt before they play. When you have felt their claws upon your flesh, not merely caught against your steel... Well. Even you might feel something.'

Only Plegua moved in silence, bringing up the rear. The Kakophoni shuddered and spasmed, his choler contained within his transfigured flesh, yet still palpably visible. Darven's death had muted the song they had shared together and now Plegua carried its melody alone.

'You will have vengeance, brother,' Eidolon promised. 'We all will.'

'The song must be appeased.' Plegua forced the words out in a breathy hiss. 'There will be a reckoning.'

A reckoning.

Eidolon smiled. The reflections that surrounded him did not return it.

The walls of the ship had transmuted once more. Gone was the impossible bone; instead it was formed of glossy black stone, flecked with motes of colour and light. The luminescence danced within the rocky prison, following them like figments and dreams. The rearing stonework reminded Eidolon of the petrified woodlands of his youth, great chasm-forests carved out and flash-frozen in the ancient wars of Strife. The noble families of Europa had claimed that things dwelt in those ruined copses, fair and yet unkind, waiting to steal away their children and leave monsters in their place.

Yet when the true monster came, with his science and his carving knives, you gave us up to him. You called slavery and hostage-taking an honour, and bade us swallow down our bile, for the sake of survival.

Eidolon viewed his life before his ascension with nothing but disdain. The rites and surgeries that had made him Astartes, made him one of the storied III, had been a catharsis. Remaking his world, so that he could bring low the stars. Weakness and foible had been banished, yet it was not until they had been reunited with the primarch that the Legion had understood what it aspired to.

Claws against his unarmoured soul, dragging him down through fire and blood and madness. Things cavorting about him in their

lunatic courts and congregations, dancing to the tune of gods and
monsters. Hungry. Forever hungering, their teeth red with his own
life's blood–

He culled the thoughts, ruthlessly. Each one was a cognitive
cancer, desperately trying to subvert his path. The past was dead.
Only the future mattered, beckoning with its burning promise.
The Throneworld would be reaved clean, reshaped by the new
desires their gods had shown them.

Eidolon sniffed the air as synaesthesia overwhelmed him,
staggering as the sensations reared suddenly and painfully.

Traitor!

The voice screamed from the blackness, almost driving Eidolon
to his knees. He let a hiss pass between his clenched teeth, looking around at the other warriors. They were already in motion.
Prepared and eager for battle. Malakris' claws snapped alight and
Vocipheron's blade swept round, already primed.

Crooning things shambled from out of the shadows, their
forms indistinct and twisted. Darkness clung to them, trailed
along like shrouds. Here and there Eidolon could still see the
marks of rank, the fragments of uniforms melted against uneven
flesh. Gold braid glimmered in the fading light, strung like a
noose around a distended throat.

They had been crew once. Lost to the warp as the ship shifted
around them, their bodies stretched like melting pict-film,
they were now barely recognisable as human. Too many teeth
gnashed in jaws that were forced to impossible dimensions,
screaming and moaning, singing with too many voices. Limbs,
bent double and rent to strange angles, clawed at the walls,
gouging the decking with relentless agitation.

The monsters filled the passageway, shoulder to shoulder,
packed in like cattle, flesh pressed against the barbed walls
and decking. Blood ran freely down their faces, smeared like
paint upon canvas.

As one, as though guided by a single consciousness, each head snapped around, milky eyes locked upon Eidolon and his men.

'We could be so much more!' they warbled, one voice ululating from their gaping mouths, projecting a wall of sound that rivalled the finest efforts of the Kakophoni. *'Embrace me!'*

The laughing guile of the daemonettes was long behind them, stripped away to only this desperate keening. The things were mere puppets now, caught in the orbit of a force greater than themselves. Knives clattered against the deck as the monstrosities dragged themselves forward, perched on stilts of repurposed bone, their every movement adding to the chorus of fugue and madness that permeated them.

They came forward in a rush of flesh, bones exposed where it had peeled back, witch-fire flaring behind their eyes or animating emptied sockets. Malakris and Vocipheron moved to meet them with a unity Eidolon had thought long since lost to them – in near-perfect concert, guarding each other's flank.

Blade and claw flared out and limbs began to tumble away, arcing through the air streaming blood and fragments of bone. Pseudopods of tortured flesh lashed for them, coiling about arms, seeking to drown them in a tide of demented skin and muscle.

The two warriors heaved two bulky, roaring creatures – bull-headed and thick-necked – to one side, impaling them to the walls. Blood boiled off around their weapons, filling the close quarters with a rancid stink.

Everything was reduced to the wet reek of sickness and mutation. All perfume and extraneous scents were forgotten, obliterated by the animal musk of the broken mortals. Eidolon spat to one side as he advanced, turning *Glory Aeterna* over in his hands.

'Is this all you have?' he laughed. 'A petty king of a paltry kingdom! Why don't you challenge me yourself?'

The monsters laughed as one, even as they began to die. Malakris drove his claws in like punch daggers, over and over, drenching himself in black blood and ash. Vocipheron took a more measured approach, each strike precisely calibrated to rend limbs from the central mass of one of the creatures.

Eidolon hefted the hammer aloft and drove it down, atomising a central monstrosity in a single stroke. Lightning whipped and crackled from the head as it continued on, through the gory remnants of the enemy, into the decking itself. The ship screamed around him, like a wounded beast, as though the guts of the *Wage of Sin* had become just as linked to the will of the Shattered King.

'He puts servants and slaves in my path because he is a coward!' Eidolon snapped. Another monster reared at him, jaws wide, spraying acid saliva. He seized it by the throat and squeezed. The monster croaked and struggled, suckered tentacles made of human meat hissing and scratching against his warped armour. They tried to claw free some of the gold that had melted and flowed along one pauldron, then fell away limply. He felt its neck snap with a satisfying crack and cast it down amongst its dying brethren.

'*No mercy, no mercy!*' the last of them called as they slunk low to the decking. Eidolon sneered and drew his pistol, aiming it directly at the massed monstrosities, begging in their weakness.

'I do not need his mercy,' Eidolon pronounced. 'I only need his death.'

The warriors passed beneath arches of human bone, carved by the hands of Legion artisans, that had now turned feral. The osseous matter had grown and swollen, spreading in questing fingers, catching the light on bladed edges like the antlers of some vast beast. Others had pushed forth like a bull's horns, or a ram's curled protrusions.

Stairs stretched out ahead of them, lit by hovering orbs of witch-fire. Eidolon pushed onwards. Up, away from them, towards the dais that surmounted the ascent.

Atop it sat a throne, carved of the same lustrous black stone, flowing back and into the meat of the ship. An indistinct figure reclined upon it. As he drew closer, Eidolon could see that it bore the shape of a warrior of the Legions, yet not clad in flesh and ceramite. It was forged from the same burning warp fire as the unnatural lanterns.

Eidolon reached to his belt and drew his pistol, holding it out as he advanced. The weapon has followed him into treachery, just as *Glory Aeterna* had. An example of ancient, priceless archeotech, lately the weapon seemed to have almost developed a mind of its own. Eidolon scarcely knew what would emit from it, only that it always brought the most exquisite deaths to his foes. That was enough, in the illuminated age they inhabited.

'Name yourself,' Eidolon said.

The thing rippled with mirth, its corpus undulating with the motion. Faces writhed within its body of flame, pushing out like captive souls seeking escape. It stood, rolling its shoulders as though it were a man.

'Am I so changed, brother?' the thing asked. It tilted its head and stepped forward. Light flowed through it, out and into the black stone of the transformed ship. The chorus of damned souls went with it, diffusing into the earth, finally granted release. The motes of light became more agitated with every step it took. *'Do you truly not know me?'*

'Some weakling brother who yearned to follow the primarch, I imagine. There are countless of them. Lotus-eating fools who would have followed Julius into yet deeper madnesses. No use at all, unless you required someone to run at the enemy screaming of their own apotheosis. You were meat, once. Now you are just a figment.'

It paused, halfway down the stairs, and let its hand close around a hovering orb of light. It looked down on Eidolon with a pose of bemused disdain, poised and ready to strike, to leap from its metres-high perch. *'You insult me, lord commander,'* it said. *'I shall no longer simply be the Shattered King. No. No longer. I shall be the mirror of the Dark Prince in their ascendancy, eternal and yet newborn. I am inevitable, unceasing. We share a common destiny.'*

'Spare me,' Eidolon sighed. 'If I have to listen to another dull idiot who believes himself to be Slaanesh caged in flesh then I might as well end myself.'

The King threw back its head and laughed. *'Perhaps you should, lord commander. Simply give in to the oblivion that you crave and–'*

Eidolon squeezed the trigger.

A beam of exotic unlight flashed out, impaling the advancing figure. The Shattered King paused but did not flinch back. Black lightning crackled across the fire of its being, before being absorbed. Darkness flickered and danced within it as it was swallowed down.

Eidolon snarled and stalked forward, holstering the pistol and bringing his hammer up with both hands. He swung it down, aiming directly for the thing's skull.

The hammer's progress stopped. Eidolon looked at the daemonic apparition, the warped reflection of what it meant to be Astartes. The Shattered King held the hammer in its precise grip, like a child holding a toy with exceptional care.

It pushed.

Eidolon flew back, almost barrelling his fellows over. He kept his footing, bracing his left leg against the glossy black stone. Light clung to him, pouring up from the scraped ground. Voices hissed in his ears, surging into his mind, seeking to overwhelm him.

Traitor.

Brother.

Murderer.

Liar.

Ghost-light after-images pulled themselves from the ground and coiled about him, weeping fire, their faces contorted in absolute agony. Eidolon pushed through them, weapon raised, *Glory Aeterna*'s light dispelling the illusory attackers. The faces of men and women snarled with animal rage and then faded away, broken by Eidolon's superior wrath.

'You are unworthy of such a gift,' the King hissed. Hands reached out, grasping for the weapon with desperate need. *'Give it to me. Lay down your burden. Surrender to the inevitable. The Dark Prince has made and remade you as a folly. A farce. You are mocked beyond the veil, mere sport for the warp's tides.'*

Eidolon's neck was thick with veins. It was not merely his gift that swelled within him now, but a true and righteous fury. That this *thing* should dare. Not a man any longer and not yet a true child of the warp. A bastard, half-breed thing. Its broken soul burning like a beacon, calling the daemonic to it, marshalling them as some unclean champion. A commander in its own right. A shadow. An echo.

He did not loose the scream.

'You talk too much,' he hissed. 'Too much for so meagre a thing.'

'I am not some little pet,' the King protested, almost petulantly gesturing with talons of fire to the gathered warriors. *'Not like them. Such pretty things, bright little souls. Perhaps they shall have a place in my court when I sit upon my throne. When I am* **as I should be.**'

'They are not for you,' Eidolon said. He stepped forwards again. Each step was agony. Not with the chaotic response of his broken form, but with the pressure the creature exerted simply by existing. He was fighting through curdled gravity, a wall of crushing fire that coiled about him, seeking entrance. Systems began to sing in his armour as it struggled to repel the flame.

He pushed onwards.

The Shattered King moved with a languid grace, almost careless as it sauntered towards Eidolon. His anger flared again. 'This is my ship. My Millennial. My–'

Eidolon's voice faltered then, choking on the words he had almost dared to utter.

My Legion.

Eidolon did not move. At his nod, the subtlest motion of his head, his warriors responded in his stead. Vocipheron advanced first, eschewing Malakris' right of rank. Instead, he stepped forth with the surety of the duellist and the oath of his blade. A fine blade, Eidolon reflected. Like *Glory Aeterna*, it was an exquisite weapon, one that had kept its keenness and its beauty even as it followed its master into betrayal. A charnabal sabre. So sharp, even now.

Eidolon watched as the swordsman raised it, pushing himself forward, swinging for the Shattered King. It growled. A blade, shadowy and indistinct, utterly at odds with the figure's burning menace, conjured to its hand. The blades met with a ringing clatter that filled the impossible space, resonating off the distant walls in ways that made Eidolon's blood sing.

Malakris, never one to be outdone, hurled himself forward, claws glittering as he swiped them down towards the spectre's head. It turned them aside, weaving between the warriors. Von Kalda fired into the melee, bolt pistol barking, uncaring whether he hit his comrades or not. They burst amidst the tumult like blooming flowers, casting fire and shrapnel about the chamber.

The room shuddered in immaterial sympathy. Eidolon finally strode back into the fray, hammer raised. Malakris' claws caught the King in the chest, while Vocipheron held its blade locked with his own. The daemonic thing hissed and spat. In the same moment as Eidolon raised his hammer, Plegua stepped out from behind him. His sonic weapon unleashed, singing its ruinous song as Eidolon brought the thunder hammer down, its crackling arc finally striking the King.

The flaming figure stiffened and cracked, more black lightning rippling across its torso as its hisses became screams. The warp earthed through it, searing lines of light moving through the black stone. It hurled its arms up and the world responded in kind.

The warriors staggered back, stumbling through the sudden rush of wind and blows of some invisible force. Malakris hurtled back, armour cracking as he impacted a glowing pillar. Vocipheron was thrown upwards, cursing as the darkness took him. Plegua and Eidolon both tumbled backwards, but at the last moment a hand snapped out and caught Eidolon about the wrist.

'*Oh, my brother,*' the King hissed. '*You do not escape me that easily!*' It pulled him backwards, into its burning embrace, as the flames surged higher and enveloped them both.

Black lightning crawled along Eidolon's armour, scouring cracks and lines of fire into the lacquer. One of the Shattered King's hands slipped down and seized for *Glory Aeterna*'s haft.

Eidolon fought. Every part of his body struggled and recoiled, and he drove a knee up and into the thing's gut. The flames rippled and surged up again. A peculiar absence of pain had begun to spread along Eidolon's arm, a numbness that crawled from where the King had reached for his hammer.

Eidolon butted his head hard against the daemonic thing and watched as it merely laughed.

Then it was gone. Eidolon whirled about. He was alone. The other warriors under his command, the great throne room… All had faded. There was only darkness and the smoky residue, the drifting, lingering mist of a dead inferno.

He staggered through the fog, swinging wildly like some inelegant berserker, cutting through the half-imagined vistas of the immaterial. Laughter chased him. Walls rose about him, indistinct as gun smoke, questing for the heavens in imitation of some distant palace.

Things moved just out of sight, darting here and there with a graceful ease, trailing iridescence through the mist. Fractals danced beyond his reach, following the revellers of the shadow hall that had ensnared him.

Eidolon could feel the thrum of the figmented reality around him, pulsing like breathing. It was as though he were trapped within the lungs of a slumbering god, his entire being encapsulated by this non-space.

Light broke the gloom in a sudden rush, and he raised a hand to shield his eyes from the power of it. Two figures gazed down at him, their silhouettes hazy in the blinding glare. One was a seated figure of golden light, radiating a cold clarity that threatened to strip away whatever pretensions he held about himself. Eidolon felt it worming into his soul, pawing at the core of his being.

The other burned with a majestic warmth, alive with the power that came only from dying to be reborn once more. Behind them the shadows moved and danced, writhing with the form of something vaster than worlds. Black fire and violet light pushed through the undulating shadow, and, for a moment, he was almost certain he could grasp what it was.

He reached out one trembling hand, but another grasped his wrist and pulled him back. Eidolon whirled, hammer striking out, hewing the empty air.

'There is always a choice,' the Shattered King whispered from all around him. Eidolon spun about again.

'Show yourself, coward!'

'Always a choice,' it repeated. *'Loyalty or treachery. Obedient*

son or warlord in your own right. I can show you the way, liberate you from the chains that bind you to petty notions. Why stand alone in service when you could rise, ascend to your true primacy?'

'I will not be a vessel for a deluded failure who lost himself to the warp.'

'Of course not,' the King whispered, almost sadly. Fingertips brushed against Eidolon's chin and the Lord Commander Primus moved, acting upon pure instinct. He shook free of the King's cloying embrace and swung the hammer around. The phantasm slid away, cloaked in smoke.

The King lunged from the opposite direction, a master of this conjured place, as one with its haunting environs. Claws thrust out like lances of fire, gouging into Eidolon's chestplate, pinning him in place.

His hearts convulsed. He could feel the vitality flowing from him, bled away by the thing's relentless and maddening assault. Colour flared behind it, as though given new strength and form from Eidolon's suffering.

He pushed back, driving his shoulder into the King's tormented corpus, forcing it back and away from him. New strength rose in his limbs, and he hefted the hammer up.

'You will never have my submission, figment,' he snarled, and swung *Glory Aeterna*.

The King flowed away and then surged in, pinning Eidolon against one of the walls. The talons bit his flank, hammering into his side again and again, till the plate rent and blood flowed down his side. Eidolon bit down hard as the pain flared bright and then faded away, siphoned and stolen by the monster's embrace.

'You,' he snarled through his gritted teeth, 'are nothing!'

He pulled the hammer round and slammed the haft into the King's chest, thrusting it back and away from him. The daemon's features split into a blazing smile again. It hurled itself forwards, desperate and puling, rabid with hunger. Eidolon hurled himself to one side, letting it rush, maddened, into the very wall it had slammed him against. The hammer came round, fully ignited, all his strength behind it.

He felt it strike something solid at last.

Reality broke around them, the black stone suddenly rushing in, a fractal nest of competing reflections, each one like a universe unto itself. The images of Eidolon cursed and howled, tearing at their own ruined flesh with taloned fingers, raking bloody lines down their skin.

He ignored them. He struck again.

The world snapped back into place around them. The other warriors looked around suddenly as their master and his opponent materialised from the roiling sea of shadow and flame. Fire gouted from a great wound in the King's flank, whipping madly as the daemonic being tried to maintain its piteous cohesion.

The King fell to its knees, flames dying upon its body. A second wave of pressure bellowed from it, driving the others back. Eidolon held firm. His grip tightened and he hefted the hammer once more. He brought it down again and again, hammering it into his foe. The fateful lightning caged within its fiery skin discharged. The reflections died – some merely going dark, where others flickered to reveal the grinning death mask of a skull.

'*Pretender prince…*' the King hissed through shattered teeth, its form reduced to a dying abstraction. The flames froze, shattered apart, ran like wax. Its features coalesced into a gurning hole in imitation of a mouth, staring with empty sockets. '*These are but the beginnings of your agonies.*'

'I have suffered longer than you can know,' Eidolon snarled. The King grinned, forcing itself up one last time. It pulled its blade free of Vocipheron's lock, as though it had merely been biding its time.

The blade lashed out, a tongue of liquid darkness. There was something familiar in its motion, in the fluid arc of it as it swung out towards him. Eidolon tried to flinch back but felt it taste blood. Armour split beneath its caress.

Instead of pulling away, Eidolon pushed forward and let it bite deeper. He savoured the agony as it pulsed through him, the gentle flow of blood down his skin.

He drove the hammer down and the King shattered. The daemon cracked into a thousand pieces, each shard of fire and madness tumbling to the decking. And it was decking again. No longer the unnatural black stone, but iron and adamantine.

Malakris laughed, the sound low and lyrical in the sudden silence of reality, mimicking the dead King's broken joy. Plegua was trilling behind them, head tilted. Listening. 'The reactors have kindled once more and the Geller field burns,' he said.

Eidolon looked at him. 'You're sure?'

Plegua nodded. 'Aye, lord. The storm abates. Soon we shall be free once more.'

The Lord Commander Primus turned his gaze to the head of his hammer. Burnt-black blood clung to it, defying the power field. The patterns it had left seemed to writhe with primal malice, a hateful intelligence lingering about the weapon like a moral stain.

'Then let us find out where we are and right our course again.'

SIX

Eidolon did not spend much time within his chambers.

The idea of rest had, at some point, become anathema to him, and the constant pain that had haunted him put paid to any fantasies of sleep.

He maintained the chambers as an affectation – a space amidst the constant madness of the ship where he could be alone and bask in that solitude. It was not enough to be a figure of awe upon the command throne. No, a true ruler maintained a distance between himself and his men.

Even upon Terra it had been the same. His family had held fortified estates, protected by myriad defence systems and men-at-arms. Their retainers had fought and died for something greater than themselves, so that some fragment of nobility could endure in that fastness which had once been a mountain.

That had been the way of Europa. Survival at any cost. Dying was for others to do. For armies and slaves. The warlords who had fought Unification and failed had done so because they thought they were the last vanguards of their way of life. In a way they had been correct. Eidolon's family, the other pretender-nobles of a dead world, had chosen a different path – yet he realised now, it had been the same.

Their children had passed beyond life and death so that they could live on. He, a second son, had been given to the flesh-smiths of the Emperor's new armies. Not to be one of the base Thunder Warriors who had smashed all resistance, not a butcher of Gaduare.

You will be an angel.

A voice brushed his mind from out of memory, and he scowled at its emergence. Too many memories, these nights. Intruding in the manner of dreams or hallucinations. A sign of weakness, if ever there was one. Perhaps when the warp's brazen excesses were banished they would cease. It was some lingering game of the Dark Prince, or of his father. Some curse of the self-proclaimed Shattered King.

You will be an angel. Who had said those words to him, so long ago? Not his father. His mother, perhaps? Some pitying sibling? One of the Emperor's agents themselves? He had been part of a golden tithe, the noble sons of Europa prostituted for the Emperor's ambitions, less than slaves, simply raw materials for the wars to come. The iron that might one day be Imperial steel. He had taken pride in that, once, long ago. Before Laeran. Before Isstvan. The parade of beautiful horrors that had led them, inexorably, to this moment.

Sons returning to murder their father. An empire on its knees. He wondered whether the Emperor had foreseen this end? Had he known, on some level, that you could not raise up a generation and turn them into weapons, into killers, into monsters, without them one day returning home to slake their appetites upon him?

Where was your foresight then? This long game, played out at last. Fate's threads come to strangle you for your hubris.

Eidolon looked up. Of all the things within his chambers, of all the trophies of war and instruments of violence, there was only one thing here that had not been utterly ruined by the gifts of the gods.

On the wall above the space where a bed would have rested, a piece of art was mounted. It had been a rendition of Chemos from the hand of Keland Roget. Beautiful, in its own way. Eidolon had savoured such things once. Mortal art had possessed an allure for him, though not in the way that it had for others amongst his Legion brothers.

He did not truly wish to create it. To possess it was enough. To know that this thing, this object, was *his*. Ownership, the desire to rule, had always been in his blood, wedded to his soul. Perhaps that was why his time with the Death Lord had been so illuminating. They were cut from the same rough cloth.

Commanders. Rulers. Conquerors.

He let his eyes trace over the curdled landscape, finding new details.

Eidolon had destroyed the piece many times since the *Maraviglia* had enlivened his soul. More times again since he had passed beyond life and death. Each time, whether he ended it by fire or blade, the piece returned. Unharmed and whole, yet changed. Sometimes a tower in the background would suddenly be made of flesh and bone. Other times there would be crucified loyalists in the foreground, close enough that the details of their fidelity could still be made out. Aquilas nailed to their chests. *Turncloak* or *Parasite* carved into their skulls.

Recently, the painting had begun to reflect a broken and burned world, teeming with desperate defenders and wrathful invaders.

Even that could be put right. When it was over, when they all sat upon their thrones, and the material and immaterial were their subjects, then there would be time for reckonings and perhaps... perhaps then for rest.

No rest for us. Not for ten thousand years of empty war. Only through me can you seize a future worth commanding.

Eidolon blinked. He turned and looked upon one of the few remaining mirrors in his chambers, its glass yet intact. The shrunken horror he had become leered back at him, its eyes brighter somehow than they had been. The rheum and cataracts had abated, leaving his sight clear. His mind was sharper, thoughts racing with all the surety of youth and vigour.

As he had once been.

He began to turn away and stopped. The reflection did not follow him. It stood and it watched, caged by glass and the gilt of the mirror. It leant forward, its eyes burning now with a predator's lustre as it drove its taloned fingers into the barrier between them.

The mirror shattered in its frame, bowing the wood and gold outwards. Slivers fell in a sudden sparkling rain, impacting the ground like bolt-shots. Most stayed in place and then began to move as the *thing* forced its way out and through, shards clinging to it, forming it, giving it life and solidity enough to lurch into the room.

Eidolon reached up and seized its throat, driving it back, snarling as he hooked the fingers of his other hand into the thing's eye sockets. It screamed with a voice of grinding glass, a silica death scream that grated against Eidolon's mind, even as molten fluid poured from the wounds. It seared his fingers, hardening and shattering almost as soon as it was shed. He hurled it backwards, and it threw out its arms, bracing itself as though against the sucking force of an airlock.

'*You cannot escape me,*' it hissed. '*We are destined for one another.*' Clawed hands closed around Eidolon's neck as it threw itself forwards in one last, desperate attack. Eidolon's hand snapped back and he drove his fist through its snarling visage. There was an explosion of fragments, wings of glass flaring up and around him. Blood stained his cheeks, hot and sudden. He flinched back and saw–

Simply the mirror, its surface now ruined as the gleaming plate lay broken into thousands of pieces. He spun about, realising he had been lost too long in fugue; that he was once again alone.

A sudden vox-click stole his attention.

'Speak.'

'My lord,' the voice crackled. 'You are required upon the bridge. There is something here that you must see.'

Eidolon strode onto the bridge and watched the madness unfold.

Everywhere there was motion. Serfs and slaves dashed around, compensating as the ship shuddered around them. Metal screamed and the air sang with machine agony. The oculus was clouded with the warp like a corpse's eye, and cracks had formed at the corners of it where the relentless pressure of the empyrean had crowded in, pushing at it through the bubble of tenuously stable reality maintained by the Geller field. He smiled at that. Even the great ship could suffer and bleed. It was, as so many things were, yet mortal.

'Why have I been summoned?' he asked, almost bored now.

The slaves bowed low, their eyes at his boots. Only the boldest of them, those still in uniform and who still held their minds, raised their hands to point beyond the fading fire at the oculus.

Out there in the darkness, there was a world.

It hovered in the infinite black, a turning orb of green seas and verdant land, a marble of contrasting beauty. His eyes caught on the swathes of white stone, visible even from orbit, that sprawled across its continents. Lights glimmered at the edges of the world, where night had already taken hold. Starlight illuminated the great expanses of the cities, beautiful in their construction.

His tongue lapped at his lips. He knew this place. Fate, circumstance, the whim and whimsy of the gods, had returned
him to this moment. He sighed. Bitterly now. He remembered,
and in that memory there was another voice, lapping at his
mind, laughing in the chambers of his soul. Mirroring his words
with dark delight.

'Tatricala.'

'There are other names, of course. Other worlds and other wars. Legions, even diminished Legions, collect accolades and stories. They collect locations. Place becomes synonymous with act. Of all the battles of the glorious and resurgent Third, and they are many now, we might think of Proxima. We lionise them there, where they earned the Palatine.

'Others might speak of the extinction of the Katara. There is a beautiful tragedy there, and were I a singer, I might commit it whole to verse. "Of the Champions in their Tumult, Of the Fall to Distant Grief."

'I am not a singer, nor a poet. I will not speak of the myriad dead, in honour or treachery. I shall not speak of the hubris of Byzas, nor any other hundred compliances. Instead, I remember Tatricala, where I watched a world kneel, and a master of men rise.'

– *Amidst the Fire: A Memoir of the Great Crusade.*
Unreleased manuscript of Kristian Partinnus,
remembrancer

ACT TWO

BODY

SEVEN

HOME AND HEARTH

Eidolon stared at the world for a long time, even as the crew quieted and his officers finally arrived.

Around the edges of the chamber, purple-clad soldiery had gathered, forming a circle of waiting warriors that sprawled to the wings of the bridge.

Where once they had worn their uniforms with pride and kept them immaculate, time had transformed them into parodies of their former grandeur. As their masters had become excessive, so they had followed. Their greatcoats were hung with gruesome trophies: artfully carved finger bones, larger scrimshawed plates of osseous matter, patterns smeared across fabric in human blood and less identifiable fluids. They had become individual works of ruinous art, each one shaped by circumstance and whim.

Once, they had been the Kalathesian 97th. Trusted, respected and taken under the wing of the III Legion. The Astartes had seen the potential in them and had nurtured it, shaping

and guiding the regiments. It had been an inevitability that
they would follow the mighty exemplars of the Emperor's Children down their path of madness and treachery.

At the centre of their gathering, their commanding officer
stood at attention, resolved not to falter under Eidolon's eye.
Lord General Stanislaus Otvar wore his desecration like a fine
suit. The metal of his ornamental breastplate had run molten,
setting into strange configurations that clung to his stout chest
like organic plates, like inlaid coral. He carried a gnarled helm
under one arm, its visage shaped into that of a snarling beast, a
carved tongue etched lasciviously across the faceplate. His free
hand was locked on the golden hilt of his sabre.

'My lord,' he made to say, but Eidolon ignored him, his sight
still focused upon the world, holding his attention rapt.

It seemed impossible. Eidolon had laughed at first, till all
about him thought him mad. He had strode from one end of
the bridge to the other, letting his gauntlets close around the
gilt of a railing. Part of him yearned to yank it free and cast it at
the oculus, or to beat some hapless slave to death. He clenched
his hands and pulled back, then let the breath hiss from him.

His choler passed and settled, like sediment within the ocean
of his severed soul.

'The gods are toying with me,' he hissed. 'Face to face with
this, of all things.'

'It is just a world,' Plegua said with a shrug. 'They break easy
enough. Nothing to fear.'

Fear. Fear. Fear. The word echoed oddly from the Kakophoni's mouth, reverberating around the bridge. Something
whispered and cajoled behind the utterance, just out of sight,
like an echo or a reflection…

'I do not fear it!' Eidolon snapped. His own gift surged out,
a booming recitation that filled the bridge space. Half-burned
banners stirred suddenly in the wind of his fury. Braziers

flickered and died. One of the mortal crew collapsed, blood running freely from their ears as they began to seize upon the decking.

'I do not fear it,' Eidolon repeated. 'It is known to me. It is where I–'

Fingers raising his face to look upon his father's glory. The smile, that welcoming smile, free from judgement or scorn. 'Rise, my son,' he says, gently and yet with such furious intensity that all around them can hear it. Like watching a sun speak. 'Rise, my lord commander.'

'Where I became who I was,' Eidolon finished.

He had been a company commander then, one of the first and the most capable. He had been leading his own detachment. A scouting force separate from both Fulgrim's attention and Lupercal's scrutiny. He had been bold, and thought himself strong, simply to have the command that he did.

Tatricala had been a world made mighty by its density. Where other polities of Old Night had sprawled outwards, assembling their petty pretender empires, Tatricala had turned inwards. It had barely exploited the system in which it lay, focused instead on crafting a martial paradise in which to bask. It had been a fortress of high ideals, stout walls and robust technology.

Eidolon had tried his best to play diplomat, but it soon became clear that Tatricala's fighting men and Council Militant would never yield to the Imperium through honeyed words alone. He had been forced, and secretly thrilled, to take up arms against them. Alone in his command, he had set about the process of assessing Tatricala's defences and fighting capability.

Before he took it apart. Expertly. Blow by blow.

All their strength at arms had ultimately meant nothing, a recurring epitaph for civilisations which met the Imperium in those glory days. Eidolon had conceived of the advance and led it to completion. Within days the Council Militant had been cast down, its armies routed, and the capital taken with surprisingly minimal loss of life. He had found the balance between bringing ruin and liberation.

At the final battle, the skies had cracked with the fire of a false dawn. The *Pride of the Emperor* had attained orbit, and the primarch himself graced them with his presence. It had been a ruse, Eidolon learned later. Fulgrim had allowed him his operational freedom to test if he was ready.

In the ashes of a culture, surrounded by those he had made subjects, Eidolon knelt as a mere legionary and rose as a lord commander.

And now the fates conspired, and he stood before it again.

Under the reflected light of the beautiful world, even the intense lumens of the bridge seemed dull. The ship's serfs gazed at it with their cattle eyes, blinking as though they could not comprehend its existence. The warp had gnawed their minds, winnowed their souls, and now the materium crashed down upon them with all its gravity.

'What is the auspex telling us?' Eidolon asked at last. The crew scrambled to answer him, fearful of his wrath as he stalked from the upper tiers, down towards his throne. Eidolon's clawed hand traced along the back of the throne, dislodging flakes of ruined gold as he gouged into the metal and stone. 'Speak, damn you!'

'Indistinct returns, lord,' one of the more minor auspex technicians chirruped. Certus, Eidolon thought his name was. The input cables flexed as he rotated to look up at Eidolon, each new processed signal sending floods of pleasure through what remained of his body. The man's eyes rolled. 'There are ships, cresting from the other side of the planet. They move in response to our presence.'

'And how many ships are with us?'

'Vox-transmissions are sporadic,' Certus mewled, stirring again as another wave of signals found his nerves. 'We have confirmation of the *Sublime Blade*, the *Broken Monarch*, *His Beauty*

Manifest, the *Dwell Eternal*, and the troop transports *Soul of Illumination*, *Trophonius*, *Refracted Sorrows* and *Benighted Agony*.'

'A fine assemblage of our strength,' Eidolon muttered. The force was enough for the task, but somehow their numbers rang hollow. Piecemeal, though he doubted there was any loyalist force in this sector cohesive enough to oppose them. Too close to Terra's major warp transits. Rogal Dorn would have pulled them all back behind his high walls and Sol's vaunted defences.

A cry rose up. 'We have clarity!' Certus strained against his bindings till flesh and wire tore, smearing the machine components with blood. The New Mechanicum adepts chittered from the dark alcoves at the bridge's edge, pleased by the profane sanctity unfolding before their optics. 'Ships, lord! Signum codes proclaim them as vessels of the Sixteenth Legion. I have– Hnn–' He paused, lost in ecstasy.

Eidolon strode forward and seized Certus by the throat, squeezing. Veins pulsed in the half-man's neck, his pupils dilating as he struggled between the pleasurable inloads and the pressure on his windpipe. 'Focus, worm!'

'The *Steadfast Spear*, the *Cthonian Kiss*, the *Solar Birthright*, and the battle-barge *Warmaster's Mercy*.'

'A strong showing in turn,' Eidolon said, nodding. He paced down towards the oculus, picking out the ships as they moved into view. How typically brutish of the Sons of Horus they seemed, their hulls scarred with kill-markings, etched into the metal, Titan-scale. Gaudy posturing and pretension, so that the Warmaster's favoured could proclaim their dominance proudly. 'Yet why do they idle? They could have torn this world from its moorings already, had they the desire. Why wait and preen in the void?'

Barbarian arrogance, perhaps, Eidolon thought with a sniff. He waved his hand in the air. 'Bring me communion. Let me speak with the representatives of our distant lord and master.'

Chuckles rose from around the bridge only to die as the hololith sparked to life.

The figure displayed was everything Eidolon had expected, and less. Armour stripped back for leanness in a reaver's manner, save where mirror coins hung from thin chains, clattering against the plate with every movement and making the audio skip. He wore his hair in a dark tangle of braids, looped with metal wire. His teeth were sharpened, and the lines of gang tattoos shimmered upon his tan skin.

'I didn't think to find some of Fulgrim's peacocks here, yet the war does keep surprising us, doesn't it?'

'I could say the same,' Eidolon said. He raised a hand and picked at his gauntlets, affecting a wearied mien. 'It's not often we see you so far from your master's skirts. True sons or false, the Warmaster likes to keep you close – whether it's his hand that guides you or Abaddon's.' Eidolon smiled. 'Perhaps it is simply the will of the gods that we find ourselves here, orbiting an unsullied world, with nothing but time running against us.'

'Gods,' the Cthonian snorted. *'You sound like Lorgar's bastards. I've had enough of gods. Violence speaks plainly enough for my liking. Maybe I'll lead with that.'* The hololithic projection stuttered momentarily and then began to speak again. *'We were following the Warmaster's main force disposition. The warp arterial…'* It paused again. *'Catastrophic immaterial collapse, so the adepts tell me.'*

'Similar circumstances to us, then. How convenient.'

Convenient, breathed a voice behind Eidolon's eyes, the ashen remonstrance of the King. **Are there any coincidences left to us, in this galaxy of fools?**

'Name yourself,' Eidolon went on, forcing himself to ignore the taunts. 'I may have spent time with the Sixteenth, but you all blend together after a while. Such similar humours.'

The warrior laughed and the hololith shook. *'I remember well*

when we had to serve as the example for the Third. So few of you…
You fought like a more numerous Legion, I'll give you that, but you
were still merely your namesake. Children.'

'We could debate ancient history until the war burns out,
cousin, or we could talk of more pressing matters. You are here.
We are here. Why? Before us lies a world. A fitting prize for any
Legion, yet you have not seen fit to claim it. Instead you sit,
warp-lost and desperate.' Eidolon brought his hand down and
tapped the row of consoles before him before looking back up
at the warrior. 'I ask again. Name yourself.'

'Gherog Sharur. Praetor of the Twenty-Third Company. We have
only just found our bearings, peacock. We barely found the world,
why would we have plans to attack it?'

'The Sixteenth are always so keen to lead from the front, to
attack first and question orders later. I would have thought you
slavering already.'

'Be silent, or I will render you so.' Gherog's image leant forward, scrutinising Eidolon. *'I don't recognise you, and if I ever did*
know you then I imagine you're too changed to match my memory.
So I extend the same question to you. Who are you, little monster?'

'I'd expect nothing less from a brash Cthonian bastard,'
Eidolon said, and yawned. 'You have the honour of addressing
Eidolon, Lord Commander Primus of the Third Legion.'

'A pretty title. Did you invent it yourself?'

Eidolon let himself chuckle at that. The sound reverberated
around the bridge and made his subordinates wince. Trans-
humans had joined the debased mortals now. His chosen
captains presented themselves as they became aware of the
brewing confrontation, recognising that a show of force was
required. An insult to one was an insult to all.

'You were the one Torgaddon humbled, were you not?' Gherog
continued.

'Murder was a long time ago,' Eidolon slurred. Despite himself he was having fun with this one. 'And I have been proven the superior warrior. After all, when Torgaddon's head came off, he did not get back up again. I did.'

'Another gift of your gods?'

'Amongst other things,' Eidolon said. 'The galaxy changes by the day. Life and death are no longer as they once were. The Phoenician has shown us as much. Just as I'm sure the Warmaster has shown you.' Eidolon's eyes had grown hooded, the dull orbs regarding the praetor with glee. 'I saw him at Ullanor. Such a burden to take onto himself. Command always is, but that level of power? It would tear anyone else apart. I suppose the constitution that a life lived amongst gang scum and failed miners conveys would be most useful, containing that much grandeur.'

'Watch your tongue, monster. The Warmaster is–'

'Glorious. Transcendent. Tediously godlike and the blade that will end the great Tyrant, and so on and so forth.' He sighed. 'I am weary of having our lords and masters, already so vaunted and potent, grow so far beyond us. Embracing the warp, becoming the godlings they always played at. Don't you yearn for something that belongs to us, before Terra is claimed? Something final. Something pure.'

Gherog's image paused and tilted its head. He clicked his tongue thoughtfully. *'What did you have in mind?'*

'This world.' Eidolon gestured. 'Rich. Verdant. Practically unspoiled. I am not sure about you, but we will require time while our Navigators decide on who will lead us onwards into the dark and towards Terra. There is opportunity here.'

'Opportunity?'

'Tatricala was a proud world in defeat, and prouder still when given the chance to rise again as part of the Imperium. It will not have turned its cloak, if it is even aware of the wider war. The Ruinstorm has isolated it. Perhaps since Calth. They may not know there are sides to be chosen,' Eidolon said. 'Regardless. We can descend. Take what we want and bear the spoils back to Terra. This place had a potency. There will be materiel we may well need, slaves aplenty. I'm surprised you haven't already tasted its promise.'

He will betray you… The voice drifted through his awareness with all the suddenness of nightmare. Eidolon looked around sharply. No one had spoken. Malakris stood and smirked. Vocipheron watched on with his quiet detachment. Plegua burbled quietly, his life made of noise and pain. None of the mortals had dared to speak. Only the shadow and the whispered hiss of the Shattered King.

Do you truly think it is coincidence that he is here?

Eidolon would not show weakness. Not here and now.

'Bring your command cadre aboard and we shall speak of the war to come.'

They hosted the Sons of Horus in the largest of the *Sin*'s audience chambers. Faded murals swept across the ceiling, Palatine Aquilae soaring amidst cracked thunderbolts and weeping stars.

Like all beautiful things upon the ship, the taint and tarnish had crept into it, ruining the wonder it had once evinced.

Under the sullied ceiling the officers of the Third Millennial gathered. Eidolon stood at the centre of them, flanked by Malakris and Vocipheron. Otvar and Plegua lurked behind them, while other soldiers of the Kalathesians had taken up their places about the edges of the chamber.

Gherog blustered into the room, all ganger swagger and unearned confidence. Two others came with him – sergeants, Eidolon assumed.

Gherog simply nodded to Eidolon. 'Tathron Vryn and Catrigos Sarek. Two of my finest.'

'I'm sure,' Eidolon said. 'Malakris and Vocipheron. Two of mine.' He stepped forward and waved a hand, triggering hidden hololithic projectors.

A world blossomed before them, born of light, orbited by visualisations of the fleet and their current dispositions.

'Tatricala,' Eidolon said. 'An early conquest of the Third. Human basic, not too dissimilar from ourselves in terms of technological ability. Lesser, of course, but a very precise form of warfare. They employed a rather remarkable commitment to defence in depth.' He waved his hand and the hololith zoomed down to the continental level. 'As can be seen here.'

The representations of the cities burned with light, each cone dense with sub-sections, hidden redoubts and plunging foundations. The cities were vast, hive-scale, yet constructed with a martial eye that would have made Dorn or Perturabo envious.

'Wonderful constructions, the great spiral cities of Tatricala. We would breach one sector, only to have the defences close around us and the enemy pour from their hidden sally-ports. There is a beautiful logic to them, once you unravel their mechanisms.' Eidolon beamed with momentary pride, his twisted features contorting with exaggerated joy. 'And we did unravel them. Not too much breaking, of course. The Mechanicum wanted to exploit so much of their old knowledge. Casualties and destruction were kept to a minimum. You would have been proud to see it, really. Elements of the dependable spear-tip assault, so beloved of your own primarch. We struck simultaneously at the three greatest cities, cut our way to their predictably insular leadership caste, and took their heads.'

'And you intend to lead its reconquest?'

'A wasteful undertaking. The age of idle crusade is at an end.' Eidolon sighed. 'We will descend, take what we need to see us to the Throneworld – slaves, materiel, and the like – and then leave them to the wretched ruin of their lives. When Terra is ours and we sweep back out into a compliant galaxy, then there will be time enough to make our mark upon it proper.'

He hesitated. He could feel the need to descend, to once again walk the surface of the world where he had... become. More than a mere twang of nostalgia. It echoed in the chambers of his soul, resonating like the music of the Kakophoni.

Gherog turned to whisper with his officers before his gaze swivelled back to Eidolon. The light of the hololith cast his features half in shadow, the crimson radiance rendering him ironically daemonic. There was no god-touched glory in Gherog or his men. They seemed to cling to the desperate physicality that they believed yet underpinned the war.

Fools. The hololith rippled and shifted. Refracted patterns of broken glass and white-hot fire flared momentarily in the furnace of artificial light. A grin made of shadows and smoke. A passing flicker of a barbed tongue moved across the projection, faded, broke apart, and was gone. *Or are they more than they appear?*

Eidolon swallowed back his bile.

If they survived to Terra, they would know all the illumination of despair. They would see what the war had become, the depths and heights of their transformed fathers. These phantasms were nothing by comparison. Hollow taunts.

Some men would break at the revelation, the warp's knowledge burning through them and leaving only bones and ashes. Perhaps the barbarian would endure a while, buoyed up by his belief in the Warmaster. Eidolon knew it for what it was. All stale promises and dead dreams. There was only whatever base pleasures could be wrung from the galaxy's corpse, bled from its occupants, sanctified in the holy obscenity that had become their lives.

He had passed far beyond belief in his father, in the Warmaster, in the truths of their arguments or convictions. Now there was only the call, the pull that echoed in his soul. Drawing him onwards, away from the morass of the past and into the fire of the future.

The first of Fabius' works. The culmination of the Laeran campaign. I am all these things and more. Evolving. How can these blunt little creatures understand what we are all becoming?

'Then show us your plan, lord commander,' Gherog growled. 'Let us see if it matches your bravado.'

Eidolon clapped his hands, and great sweeps of light arced across the image at his signal. There were six in total, vast assault projections that at once encircled the enemy and drove in to overwhelm them. The tiered fortresses of the Tatricalans were surmounted and surrounded, harried by fast assault units even as they were buffeted by massed armour. A storm of sea green and ruined purple consumed them, burning them down to nothing.

'Our primary target should be the Palace Militant,' Eidolon began to explain. 'The seat of their government and whatever Imperial command remains. The other cities will be less challenging, yet will bear sizeable rewards in their own way. An even-handed state of affairs,' he stated proudly. 'Assuming you have the manpower to back it up, of course.'

'We do,' Gherog snapped back. His warriors jostled forwards to his side, hands upon their weapons. Eidolon stepped forth to meet them, weaponless, arms raised. Gherog was face to face with him now, his own hands still at his side, balled into fists. 'You presume much here, lord commander.'

A shadow moved behind Gherog, drawing Eidolon's eye. Motes of flame trailed through the air like shed feathers, drifting just out of sight. The reflections in the gloss of the walls were not returning his gaze.

We all serve our masters… the King whispered. Eidolon forced himself to ignore it, to respond as befitted his station.

'As is my right. Enforced by the fact I could crush you like the gutter worm you are.'

'You could try,' Gherog said with a nod, rolling his shoulders as he did. 'But I would hate to make you uglier than you already are, monster.'

'Promises will get you nowhere so long as they are idle.' Gherog glared in response and Eidolon stepped back, letting his fingers drift into the hololith, intertwining his claws into the midst of the war to come. 'Return to your ships and make ready. When the skies of this world burn with the phoenix's wings, then you may commit your rabble.'

EIGHT

THE VICTORY TO COME

The skies above Roshan had caught fire, in the hours just before dawn.

Roused from his barracks, Colonel Haslach had thought it *was* merely the rise of the sun. Till he had checked the chrono. The false dawn stretched across the horizon, a great sweep of light and fury. Crimson and umber warred amidst the black of the night and the distant light of the stars.

Some of the stars, he noticed, had begun to move. Stars that had not been there the night previously. Many of his company had wept, not with fear but with relief.

The Imperium, they had said, over and over. *The Imperium's come back for us. We are not forgotten.*

We are not forgotten.

Colonel Haslach had swallowed deep at those words and turned away so that his men could not see his face, or the sudden fear which dwelt there now. *How can we be certain we have been found by the right side?*

He had quit the walls shortly after that, intent on not giving the burning horizon the attention it so brazenly demanded. He had made his way down through the many flights of stairs, out into one of the vast courtyards of the Palace Militant. Time had changed the purpose of the citadel, but the name had lingered.

He wondered if one day the iterators and bureaucrats would finally change it to something more becoming of the Imperium as it would be. Soon, they promised, there would be an end to war. An end to the tithes of flesh and resources. When the galaxy was compliant, and the Emperor's dominion was absolute, then all the plenty of the cosmos would cascade down upon them. They would have new opportunities, at home and abroad. Not merely to serve and fight and die, but to thrive.

Years ago the prop-screeds had talked of the opportunities in the east, of Ultramar rising. Haslach knew in his soul that he would never see it. He would never leave this world as anything other than a soldier. There was a certain comfort in that. His family had served as Tatricalan Wallsmen for generations without fail. Mothers and fathers, brothers and sisters, all had done their part to ensure the continuity of their civilisation.

We endure so that all of Tatricala might survive, his father had always said. A mantra engraved on the man's heart, carved into his very being by years of loyal service. Their masters had changed, true enough, but Haslach knew in his own heart that their determination remained as strong.

Did it matter that there were fewer bodies upon the walls when the Imperium had sworn to keep them safe? That their children were raised up to Imperial Army regiments rather than given their places within the civil defence corps? He did not know. Such questions remained forever beyond him, and the iterators were always present with their guidance.

The III Legion had left many examples of Imperial artists and philosophers with the Tatricalans after the liberation, the better to bed down the ideas of Terran culture. In time, they assured, it would become galactic culture. *Human culture*. All would be the Imperium and all the petty divergences of Strife would be set aside and rectified. The Emperor, beloved by all in His infinite mercy and wisdom, had already planned for it.

He had wanted desperately to trust in such pronouncements. That there was a plan guiding them in the infinite randomness of the universe. He heard the whispers in the shadows of the *Lectitio Divinitatus* and had ignored them. Haslach didn't need a god. There *were* no gods. Mortal might and will shaped the galaxy now.

He idled in Liberation Square, distracted again by thoughts of the Imperium – if it was truly the Imperium – returning. A tawdry name for the monument that had risen in the wake of the Great Crusade. A semicircle of marble columns reared up from a central platform of black volcanic stone. Arrayed around the base of each column were beautifully rendered golden statues, each one depicting a warrior of the Legion that had illuminated Tatricala.

Haslach had passed this way many times during his life, making the square into a central cog of the machinery of his days. He drew nearer, gazing up at the renditions of the Astartes.

And their master.

Below the central column were two figures, their gold filigreed with platinum and inlaid with precious jewels. The larger figure was truly immense, a looming presence that dominated even the great open space of the square. Its power and majesty dwarfed even the mighty rendering of an Astartes that knelt before him, marked with rank carvings and intended for some greatness.

It evinced strong and strange emotions in him. He took in every detail, as he always did. The statues were beautiful in such a way that he always found new facets to admire, things he had never noticed before. Like a secret slowly being unravelled before his eyes.

Noble, inspirational figures. Protection from the xenos threats and rebellious elements that lurked beyond the sky. Then the storms had come, and the silence. No ships and no astropathic messages. Only the dark and the cold, closing in about them, smothering them in its unending bleakness.

The thought had haunted them – that they might die alone and unmourned. Many had gone mad and taken their own lives rather than force the slow starvation that might come without Imperial plenty. An empire half built and a culture half demolished, striving for simple survival.

Haslach suppressed a shiver. He tried to focus on the sculptures again, the curve of their features, the immensity of them. At once comprehensible and yet vaster than worlds, too mighty for the confines of Tatricala. He measured himself against their grandeur. He was no longer a young man, and clinging to a post that the years had diminished. There was grey creeping in at his temples, and his aim was no longer what it used to be. Yet he still had his mind, kept sharp by duty and relentlessly honed under the state of emergency they had endured these last years.

The storms had passed, yet the fear lingered. It clung to everything, smothering the world like the gilding of the square. Now there was fire on the horizon, and the twin serpents of hope and doubt were once again writhing in his belly.

The first sirens made his head snap round, the statues forgotten as he staggered in near-physical shock. The clatter of anti-aircraft weaponry realigning rang through the square. His eyes rose to the walls, to the men already moving in their own sudden bursts of momentum. He started to move, stumbling over his own feet.

The first shells began to stain the air. Fire and flak hurled itself into the darkness, seeking targets that never appeared. He could hear confused shouts for clarification, for orders. His vox clicked from channel to channel, before it chirruped with a priority override. One of his opposite numbers from another city… He listened again to the ident-code. It was from Sartros. Down in the equatorial zones. He keyed into the channel.

Only screams greeted him.

The vox-capture mechanisms had been set on a wide band, taking in every moment of human agony as it was splayed across the city's skin. He could hear the population dying, a culture being wiped out. Wet tearing sounds echoed into his ear, undercut again and again by undiluted, unfiltered pain.

'Children of the Emperor,' a voice rumbled over the vox, booming with laughter. *'Death to His foes!'* The sharp reports of bolter fire drowned out the noise before the crunch of a descending boot finally silenced the transmission.

As though rushing in to fill the silence, the air around him was suddenly screaming. Haslach staggered back, eyes up, watching as the first ships tore overhead. The walls were burning as munitions rained. He saw men, men that he knew, that he had served with for years, reduced to nothing more than silhouettes against the firestorm.

The flames caught on the edges of the howling ships, illuminating the corroded metal, the strangely warped hulls with their eye-searing colours and the lurid murals that still glistened wetly there, as though freshly painted. A great talon and the sweep of a wing.

A second wave swung in low again. Explosions rocked the great slab-sided buildings behind Haslach as he turned. His hand was on his sidearm as he screamed orders into the vox that would never reach his men.

'Form up! Eyes on the enemy! Weapons ready! Form up, men!'

The roar of the great ships was everywhere around him now,

consuming the world in its cacophony. He turned to run when an almighty crash rang out behind him. Shrapnel and debris struck his back. Blood blossomed along one cheek, and he winced back.

He hit something solid and turned slowly.

The figure that had struck the earth towered over him, as massive as one of the statues. A twisted mockery, its nobility distorted. Pale hair clung lankly to one side of its head, its flesh pulsing and writhing with some internal motion. Its armour was a molten ruin of pink and gold, broken only where other riotous colours had been smeared, or had emerged from the metalwork of their own volition. It clung to an immense hammer, its head wreathed in killing lightning.

The monster's mouth twisted into the semblance of a smile, and it raised the weapon.

'Death to His foes,' it repeated, and brought the hammer down.

Eidolon looked down at the slurry he had reduced the soldier to, poking at the human detritus with one boot before turning away.

The galaxy teemed with prey, with precious little toys the gods had prepared for them, yet they broke so easily. From Isstvan to Terra, humanity was an eternally frail disappointment. Eidolon despaired that he had ever been so weak and fragile. If he had not ascended, would he have lived the same short and stunted life, content to die for his family's honour rather than be offered up as a sacrifice to the Emperor?

Unity made me what I am, but it could just as easily have broken me…

He turned away from the shattered corpse and looked up at the centrepiece of the city's petty veneration. One of the columns had already been struck by missile fire, crumbling away, half of it jutting from the pavilion like a shattered spur of bone. He stalked forward, turning the hammer's weight over and over in one hand.

The statue of Fulgrim looked down at him, seeing him with the same dulled metal eyes and simpering praise as it spared for Eidolon's simulacrum. He stepped towards it, reaching out one clawed hand to draw his fingers along the lines of the sculpture.

He remembered when it had been raised. The finest artisans of the fleet had toiled for weeks to craft something worthy of the Phoenician's image.

I wanted to commemorate the occasion… Eidolon's gene-father whispered from out of memory. *The generations to come must see the faces of those who liberated them. We raised them up, my son. We gave them unity.*

His hands clenched around the haft of *Glory Aeterna* and he raised it in one sharp motion. He snarled as he brought it down. Metal splintered and buckled. His own once-perfect face shattered under the blow. Features deformed and ran as the fielded hammer struck it. The metal melted and pooled as he destroyed the shadow of his former self.

Eidolon growled and then paused, leaning his hammer into the molten wreckage and steaming shards, the air wafting with atomised metal. He turned and looked at Fulgrim, his gauntlets still locked around the hammer's haft.

It would be so easy. To destroy your legacy as well. Perhaps mine will suffice for now.

Eidolon turned away from his father's idol in disgust and surveyed the burning city. He had dropped into the heart of it, to honour the reconsecration of the square and smear its ashes upon the heart of his old pride. Around him, other elements of the Third Millennial were deploying. Malakris' men whooped with savage joy as they lunged from the gunships or burst from the barbed cocoons of the Kharybdis and Dreadclaw assault craft. One of the Dreadclaws impacted hard against a central spire, claws scrabbling for purchase as its melta-cutters and drills began to incise their way into the city's flesh.

They were murdering a culture. Bit by bit. Action by action, they were forcing a civilisation's face into its own rancid blood. They were killing the future.

The human race's fate was a single, drawn-out scream, milked from lungs already choked with their own deaths.

They were still illuminators. They still brought the light and promise of what was to come. Just as the aeldari had realised what they were bringing into being.

Eidolon let himself laugh. That had been their end. The death of all they had been. Humanity might well follow them to that grave. Perhaps he was ensuring its end, even now. Digging the charnel pits for worlds he would never know. People he would have no kinship with.

When Terra was theirs...

When Terra is ours...

Then what?

He paused. There was nothing here that could truly hurt him. Not yet. He could hear the roar of sonic weapons upon the walls as the Kakophoni unleashed themselves. He fancied he could even hear the clatter of blades as Vocipheron's aesthetes sated their martial pleasures. Duels would be ringing out across the burning city. A fine dirge to wing the mortal chattel to their deaths or their enslavement.

Perhaps, if he listened then he would hear the Cthonians as their own attack vectors swept in, the whoops and jeers of ganger savagery, elevated to the transhuman. There was an ember of nobility somewhere in Eidolon's heart that still recoiled at their very existence.

When this world burned and all had been taken to slake the appetites and needs of the III, then he could dwell on such things. Eidolon knew in his heart that they would have their place above all the others, even if it took ten thousand years to attain it.

'Perhaps I will deal with you later, father,' he said to the statue, before he turned and began to idle towards the waiting command centre. 'I have other matters to attend to. I have a world to murder.'

NINE

WHISPERS OF RUIN

Listen.

The voice whispered from every corner, every shadow and flicker of flame. It danced through the dying city like a promise, and only those blessed of the Legion were entitled to hear its song.

Listen.

Malakris' claws had been gore-slicked when he began to kill. He had taken to the fray with the weapons unpowered, cleaving through mortal soldiers with minimal effort. He enjoyed watching as they died, eyes wide with pain and shock, denied the quicker death that power-fielded weapons would convey.

Occasionally he stopped to lap at the blades, his dark tongue slipping out to drink the lives of his victims. Each one had its own subtle bouquet. The hints of a life lived, the spice of mortal fear and panic. Who was a drunk or an addict. Which of them carried a genetic poison that would one day blossom to the fore – as a toxic legacy for their children or the blossoming canker from within.

Malakris tasted their being, their very souls, through their spilled blood. He laughed as he killed. He had always enjoyed the act. He would not deny it now. Murder had become as easy to him as breathing, a reflex, an afterthought.

His armour clicked and clattered as he moved. He had taken time with the Techmarines and the Mechanicum to augment it. Now it truly fitted him. It moulded to him, bound to him as the second skin it ought to be, its barbs biting into his flesh and incising him in ways that generated the most exquisite pain.

Listen!

He paused in his revels. Las-fire pattered uselessly off his armour as he strode onwards and finally ignited his claws. Unclean light stained the air as the defenders rushed in closer. Malakris was bored now. The world offered very little challenge to him. He might as well have allowed the Kalathesians to have their fill.

He took his time with them, letting the Wallsmen achieve some paltry easy hits. A pivot that brought him into the line of fire. A false recoil here, a faltering step there. It was all theatre in the end.

They charged him now, the brave fools. Malakris raised one clawed hand at his head and saluted them. A missile streaked from overhead, and he sidestepped it, the detonation jostling him to the side. The fire rendered him as a black void before the eyes of the soldiers, a looming shadow, barbed and ominous, lit only by the hellish conflagration and the murderous flare of his own claws.

'This is the inferno you have made for yourselves!' he called, broadcasting aloud now. 'The Lord Commander Primus' pleasure is upon you, and I am his red right hand!'

'For the Emperor!' someone screamed in desperation, and the charge continued on. He watched them as they surged forward, their fatigues muddy brown and their breastplates dull steel, like a flash-flood of brackish water. Moribund little creatures. They had built their high walls and were content to cower behind them, becoming merely a part of the stonework. They might as well have been entombed living within the great defences, brick and mortar for a future already dead.

The officers knew that they would not kill him alone, and so the first waves were mere Army troopers. Lasguns firing. Bolts straining to pierce his armour. He could see they were already overcharged, their cells burning out so very quickly. Guttering candles in the cruel dark.

Bayonets glinted in the firelight as the soldiers surmounted ridges made of broken paving stones, tripping over the uneven edges, vaulting across toppled columns. Malakris wondered at the arithmetic they had undoubtedly employed. How many human-standard soldiers it would take to lay low a single legionary.

More las-fire pattered against his armour. A solid shell struck the side of his helm, staggering him for an instant. He growled and let his claws click together. They were nothing, and yet their sheer determination was a wearying thing.

He lunged forward into the thick of them. Even well prepared, they were still shocked at his movements. He took pleasure in the transhuman dread flashing across their faces, even if only for a moment. They were committed now. Both of them locked together. They could fight the monster suddenly amongst them, or they could die.

The blades at the ends of the enemy guns sought his flesh, blunting and breaking against his armour. Heavier weapons found him. Bolter emplacements and plasma guns turned the air to fire and shrapnel around him. Stone shattered and burned. Dust and sand became glass in the sudden heat, even as the enemy dead were atomised or flash-seared. A heavy bolter shell cracked against his breastplate and drove him back. He felt something hot run down the inside of his armour, and he relished the creeping sensation.

The stink of cooked human meat filled his nostrils, even through the filters of his raptor-faced helm. He roared and the sound boomed out over the battlefield in a wave. Amplified, but not to the dizzying heights of Eidolon or his Kakophoni. Enough to wrong-foot and intimidate, not to break bones.

'Now,' he signalled.

The scream of jet thrusters cut through even the din of battle as the other members of his squad tore overhead. The assault legionaries howled into the melee, chainblades roaring and bolt pistols snarling. Men came apart in welters of gore, opened from crown to groin, bisected outright, heads and limbs cloven free as they set about their bloody work.

'*Well baited, captain!*' voxed Rykan Bail, his second. A finer devotee of the paths of pain he had yet to encounter. '*The vermin scatter! We should chase them into their holes, dig them out and crucify them for the amusement of the men! Pin them screaming upon the walls as a warning to all the others! Flense them living and–*'

Malakris cut off the stream of suggestions, content to relish his own murderous pursuits. One of the Wallsmen was crawling away from him, his legs broken by the landings. The man was dragging his body along, clawing onwards through the wreckage, his fingertips reduced to bloody stumps. Malakris moved after him, watching him like a child would observe a wounded insect.

Listen!

The voice was purring at the back of his mind again, insistent and direct, so very familiar. If he focused, he could finally know who it was that spoke to him with such absolute authority. The commanding presence that haunted him, that spoke in his dreams and his waking hours. That urged him towards greater and greater excesses.

He reached down and seized the mortal by the head, lifting him up bodily. He began to squeeze. He felt the armoured helm crack and fall away. He felt flesh part and bones break. He could practically taste the marrow as it was released from the thin shell of the man's skull. Then the raw brain meat fell out and away, cooking to dust against the power-fielded claws.

He let out a ragged sigh of satisfaction. His flesh crawled with contradictory emotions, his nerves saturated in obscene pleasure. His soul was singing, caged in his own body, pounding alongside his hearts within the plate of his fused ribcage.

Malakris looked up suddenly.

A shadow stood silhouetted against the burning skies, cloak fluttering in the sudden rush of furnace winds. He knew its shape. He knew its intent. It was Eidolon, impossible as it seemed. Gesturing with one clawed hand, the light behind him making him seem to burn with black flame, caught in the killing breeze.

Malakris bounded up the rise and stared over the edge. Below them the Sons of Horus marched, their ranks maintaining far more cohesion than the broken warbands of the III. Most of their shots found their mark with a crude efficiency.

Methodical. Clinging to their orders as if they could protect them from the flood. The voice was eager at his ear again.

All it would take was the slightest of gestures, the most miniscule of efforts, and there could be a sacrifice worthy of his ascension.

They do not deserve your majesty or might. Show them what you can be. Do what must be done. In my name.

'I'm listening now,' Malakris breathed, his eyes rising skyward as the gunships of the XVI hurtled overhead. 'I'm listening, lord.'

They died like cattle and there was no sport in it, no joy.

Even the officers had put up little to no fight, and Vocipheron despaired of it. Was this the calibre of men they had left in their shadow? Curs who set their subordinates against the Legion? Who would sacrifice countless others to save their own selfish skins?

He fought through the burning ruins that had once been a military scholam, the seared remains of desks and parchment stirring at his feet. Ashes clung to everything, both the flaking detritus of burning wood and the oily soot of atomised bodies. Vocipheron had paused amidst the horror to clean his blade, its edge clotted with blood and flesh, depositing it in a wet pile at his feet. He tossed aside the rag that had once been a uniform and let it burn.

Let it all burn.

He winced away from the thought, alien and sudden as it had come. He was not some craven Destroyer, to obliterate the world merely so he could say he had won. Leave that to the vulgar Legions, the mad and the depraved. He would not count himself amongst their number. He would burn himself before he descended to such a depth. Yet the thought was insistent and pervasive. The world yearned to burn, to be destroyed and remade. Only from the ashes could the phoenix truly arise. Chemos had been a dead cradle, and yet Fulgrim had brought it life once more.

'With me!' he called. More of his chosen blades rushed to join him, hurling themselves over rough-hewn barricades. Toppled columns lay across the great avenues, hewn down like dead trees to stymie the advance of a Legion force. Already they were stained and smeared with blood and viscera, patterns emergent within the bloodshed.

Vocipheron forged on, out of one barracks and into the vastness of an auditorium hall. His vox crackled as the other, more distant warriors of his unit, his Blade-sworn, reported in. Fighting their individual wars, the lonely pursuits of the duellist.

'No true challenges yet,' huffed Alef Catragani, one of Voci-pheron's comrades-in-arms. 'It is like fighting mere recruits. Give me the Sons of Horus any day, or even Malakris' rabble.' He looked askance at Vocipheron. Like his master, Alef main-tained discipline of the flesh. He was unscarred and his hair tumbled down his shoulders in a great spray of ivory. 'You should be ending your rivalry in blood. The captaincy could be yours, if you would but seize it.'

'A fine undertaking in a warzone,' he grumbled. 'There will be time enough for that later. I will give him a gutter death, just as he deserves, but in my own time. By my blade.'

Alef shrugged and staggered away, intent on finding worthier prey. Vocipheron's instructions had conveyed an impressive independence in his men. As it should be.

They had been raised up by his own hand. Chosen from the ranks of the Third Millennial for their martial skill and abso-lute detachment. Free from the wider taint of the Legion, spared from the worst excesses. He had killed those who did not meet his high standards and expectations himself, blade to blade.

Vocipheron did not consider himself a Lucius or a Cyrius, or any of the other masters of the blade whom the Legion spawned in multitudes. Too many laid claim to such lofty heights, meas-uring themselves against external standards instead of focusing upon the purity of the craft. Even if he could never best them, he knew that he had dedicated himself utterly to his chosen path.

He brushed his free hand along the surface of his armour, fingers tracing along the gilded cracks in his plate. Every wound was honoured and repaid, every slight avenged. When the deeds were done, he would prepare and melt the gold him-self, working it into the armour along with the ceramite sealant.

He was becoming art.

A battle cry cut through the smoke as one of the officers

finally committed herself to the game. Vocipheron smiled. He wore no helm, so the woman could see the face of the man who would end her. The other warriors fell back, silent and grinning.

He brought his sabre up, the gilded hilt sparkling in the half-light.

'Well met, daughter of the Imperium. I am Vocipheron, blademaster of the Third. I would have the honour of your name before I end you.'

She spat at the ground. There was blood on her pale cheeks and in her dark hair. The light of her own powered blade cast her in a pool of illumination, as though singling her out for his attention. The woman stood tall and lean, a soldier's build. A professional, though not a challenge.

'Cerel, fiend.' She practically hissed the words at him. 'I stand as a captain of the Wallsmen.'

'While you still had walls,' he allowed, softly, almost gently. Her face twisted with anger.

'Why would you do this? You once liberated and defended this world. Now you tear it down in a single night of bloodshed and madness.'

'I wish you could understand,' he said, and was surprised to find he meant it. 'The Emperor's lies have set this galaxy in chains. They will be broken. World by world and wall by wall. All the way back to the Throneworld and the Palace.'

'You'll be stopped. Perhaps not here, but you will not succeed.'

He paused and sighed, rolling his shoulders and raising his own blade. 'Perhaps not, captain.'

Perfection waits if you would but seize it. Surrender. Once your rival is gone, nothing shall stop your rise. Let this world burn and we shall rise together from the ashes!

The voice, the whisper, made his fingers clench around the hilt. She roared with anger and pain and threw herself forwards. He sidestepped her clumsy blow, feeling a strange uncertainty creep in. She spun and swiped at him, even as he flinched back and away. He brought his own sword round and down. Cerel turned her blade over and blocked the strike, but her limited skill could not blunt the transhuman strength behind the blow and she practically folded, forced down till her knees scraped at the ground and she let out a wretched howl of pain.

'Up,' he said, stepping back, drawing his blade away from hers. She forced herself up and spun around, slashing at him again. One great hand closed around her wrist. A flick of it and she screamed, the bones broken. He moved forward and brought his own sabre up to her neck.

'Even the least of warriors deserves to die on their feet,' he whispered, and then drove the charnabal steel through to the bone.

The walls were burning and falling, echoing about Til Plegua like a song.

The Ruin-singer shambled along the battlements, driving the mortal chattel before him in a fear-panicked herd. He grumbled and chanted as he did, the sound reverberating around the walls, ringing like the tolling of distant bells. Omens of doom, signifiers of the end that had come.

Many of the brothers of the III had been transformed, yet none to the extent of the Kakophoni. The *Maraviglia*'s poison song had found them, metastasising from the temple above Laeran to lodge in their souls, like a spiritual pestilence, a relentless carcinoma. Beyond that it was an addiction, born of the Dark Prince, cast out into an uncaring universe to ensnare those who possessed *vision* above all else.

When the voice spoke to him from the shadows in its many voices – as the thousand whispers of Slaanesh, as the primarch's honeyed tones, in the voice of the Lord Commander Primus – he ignored it. It was nothing. Merely notes in the song. More voices in the Eternal Chorus.

They held no purchase upon him or his brothers.

They fought with graceless individuality, each one taking their own liberties and indulgences. Men were cast screaming from the walls or blown apart in the sonic refrain of their weapons. Their voices rose with the great instruments they wielded, just as capable of tearing their enemies apart. That was why they had been made – to kill their enemies, to bring a galaxy to heel. The difference was that now, in their freedom, they were able to savour it.

His fingers deftly worked over the dials and levers of his weapon, sliding to press keys and pull at trigger points. He coaxed another sonic blast from it, rending a Wallsman apart limb from limb. Blood and viscera rained off the wall, coating another tier of defenders in gore. His laughter now was sick, slick and booming.

Out on the verdant plains the artillery was finally finding its range, the booming reports adding to the symphony being born about Plegua and his men. Closer in, Legion Fellblades were opening fire, hewing into the outer walls till the flames climbed high, buoyed up by the melting stonework and running metal.

Around them a culture was dying, being ground down to nothing. They had reports, howling and whooping over the vox, of massed engagements across all the great Tatricalan cities. Spiralling their way towards this vast fortress in a war of annihilation, decimating them by degrees.

The screams of the dying were thick upon the air. Soldiers and civilians alike expired at the end of XVI Legion guns or came face to face with the atrocity offered by the III.

Every new addition to the song, each permutation of its melody, thrilled Plegua and drove him onwards to new heights of exaltation and atrocity.

He hesitated as he moved along the wall, looking down at the pinned form of a Wallsmen soldier. A stray blast of sonic purity had toppled a defensive alcove, crushing his legs beneath iron and masonry. Plegua tilted his head, savouring the moment that the man finally noticed him through the fog of agony and began to stir and scream.

Plegua reached down to his belt and unhooked a blade, a simple flensing knife. An instrument of artistry, just as treasured as his mighty instrument-weapon. He leant in, the charnel perfume of his breath close enough that the man could smell the death that had come for him.

Plegua ripped back the uniform with one immense hand, pressing down upon the pale, blood-streaked flesh below, like a sculptor evaluating a block of marble.

'Do not worry, little mortal,' he murmured, distracted as he began to cut – as he began to milk the man's howls into the glory of the ever-louder song. 'I am not here simply to make you suffer. I am here to make you sing.'

By the time he was done, the whispers were barely even that. They held no power over him. They found no purchase. There was only the glorious ruin of the Dark Prince's aria.

TEN

THE HEART OF ALL THINGS

The command centre was already dying around him, wracked by the systemic shock of the invasion and the violent spear-tip assault of the XVI.

Black iron and rough stone had formed the walls and corridors, at first, in the earliest days of Strife. Time had sharpened the structure, shaping it until it had become a winding labyrinth, the only guides being the dull metal glyphs that crawled along the tops of the walls.

Gothic had replaced them in places, but it had been a hollow effort. Half-born and fleeting. Now to be shunted aside and burned clean.

Eidolon strode through the corridors as though he already owned them, the air thick with smoke and the stench of dying men. Around him the cogitators were failing, forcing out their last susurrus of binharic expressions. He let his fingers drift across them, displacing dust and ashes. The corridor was braced by plasteel beams, straining as the fortress died above them. He could already scent the weakness infecting them, the rigours that would bring them to ruin.

The heart of the Palace Militant, of the great fortress city, the heart of all things, was close around him. Its dimensions had not been fashioned for the Astartes physique, nor had conquest altered them to fit their liberators. Eidolon ducked his head, his augmented bulk filling doorways as he moved ever closer to his target. Crimson emergency lighting flooded the passageways as readily as the smoke, lending it a hellish light.

It reminded him of ships during void combat, ailing and lance-struck. Worlds died slower than ships, but just as intimately. Eidolon had fought in many different circumstances, across the galaxy's span. Worlds of bitter cold and burning sand, dead worlds peopled only by ghosts and murdered dreams, stations and ships of the Imperium and its alien enemies. It was all the same, in the end. For all the variety the galaxy offered up, there was only the familiarity of war. The same refrain, played out over and over. From Terra to the edge of the known, and back again.

A senior Wallsman rounded the corner, streaked with soot and blood. Brocade glimmered dully on his shoulders, a mantle of authority. He started when he saw Eidolon, alone and monstrous, towering above him, head scraping at the ceiling. Eidolon hunched low, providing the man a better look in the low red light. His smile was bloodied in the gloom as he lurched forward, like a revenant or ghoul from out of legend.

The man fired. One bolt-round went wide and the other ricocheted harmlessly off one immense pauldron. The third and fourth hit him in the breastplate, and he staggered backwards momentarily. He laughed as the pain ebbed through him, warring with the flow of pleasure. He raised his gun and fired, barely even bothering to sight the shot.

The capricious weapon bathed the enemy soldier in a wave

of garish green light. The rad-shot's volatile atomics disintegrated his flesh with a crackling flash, searing his shadow onto the wall behind him. Eidolon moved onwards, past the bleak memorial, rounding the corner and striding into the beating heart of the command centre.

New klaxons were sounding at the rad-burst, harsh alarms shrilling while the hydraulics whined in the walls and the blast doors struggled to close in response to the toxic discharge. Denied power, contradictory messages flooding their systems, the great bastion's defences were sluggish. He stopped and bent low, reaching up with a free hand to hold the ailing door up, pushing it back into place as he emerged into the command centre proper.

It was already mortally wounded. Bodies lay piecemeal, scattered about the chamber by furious chainsword swipes. Heads had been impaled upon the men's own bayonets, thrusting up from the top of the cogitator consoles and hololith tables in a grim tableau. Those who had prepared such a display were still here, idling in the ruin they had crafted.

Six warriors of the Sons of Horus stood in a semicircle, their weapons held ready, with another at the centre of them, three paces ahead. He turned as Eidolon entered, removing his helm and tossing it casually onto one of the nearby benches. It knocked against a disembowelled body, making the entrails slip to the ground in a wet, unwinding rush.

Gherog Sharur looked at Eidolon with open disdain and spat to one side, letting the acidic saliva sizzle against the steel flooring.

'Lord Commander Primus,' he shouted. 'I'm surprised you made it through without all your pretty little captains.'

'Always pleased to surprise you, captain,' Eidolon replied, resting his hammer against the edge of one of the last working cogitators. He pressed down, indenting the metal of the machine, milking frenzied data-screams from its suffering machine spirits.

He looked around at the slaughter. 'Efficiently done,' he said with a smile, 'though it lacks a certain artistry, I find.'

'We've seen what passes for your art,' hissed one of the Cthonians. He wore the markings of a chieftain and, even helmed, palpable loathing bled from him. Ornamental fangs glimmered on the faceplate of his helm, forming a wolfish snarl. Mirror coins hung from chains about his pauldrons, amidst the carved kill-marks. Gangish scrawls had been beaten, etched and painted into the metal, rendering it in almost Damascene sworls of brazenly displayed allegiance. He was a living talisman, a totem of distant and besieged Cthonia.

'I would know the name of the one who questions me,' Eidolon sighed.

'Annungal,' the man growled. 'Chieftain and champion of the Sixteenth. Beloved of the Warmaster.'

'I'm sure you are,' Eidolon drawled. 'As beloved as I am by my own primarch.'

'Stop taunting my men, monster,' Gherog said, glowering at Eidolon. 'I won't be able to stop them if they decide to put you in your place.'

'Any warrior of yours that raises a hand against me shall lose it,' Eidolon promised. 'I have no compunction against reducing any of your fine soldiers to red mist and entrails. There won't be enough left to make sport of, let alone art.'

'Pretty threats, from one of Fulgrim's dandies,' Annungal spat. 'The Warmaster–'

'The Warmaster is not here,' Eidolon said. 'Neither is the Phoenician. We are simply abandoned sons, stranded by circumstance. What comes next is our own affair.' He threw his arms wide. 'And behold, the initial thrust of the spear, claiming the enemy's heart while I can only look on.' He paused. 'While my men cleanse the cities and take their spoils. Slaves, materiel, enough to propel us onwards to Terra itself.'

'Spoils we will all share in,' Gherog said carefully.

'But of course,' Eidolon agreed with a slack smile. 'All shall be needed by the bitter end. Our fathers shall not fight alone. All strength shall be required. It is my honour, and my privilege, to bear the Third Millennial towards our final confrontation. That is what good leadership exists for.' He turned the hammer over again, tapping it against the cogitators. 'Already my favoured warriors are gutting the enemy's defences and breaking their resistance.' He made a show of looking around. 'I had hoped to take their surrender personally, but you seem to have made that decision for them.'

Gherog shrugged. 'Didn't seem worth the words.'

'It rarely is with you bold Cthonians,' Eidolon tittered. 'Do you think your Warmaster will love you more for your untrammelled violence?'

'It doesn't matter if he does,' Gherog said. 'We will go to him blooded and unbowed. His warriors. His champions. We' – he struck his gauntlet against his breastplate – 'are the elite. The Warmaster's own. I would scour this world to ashes and piss on what remained if it pleased him.'

'You still think yourselves so mighty?' Eidolon asked with genuine interest. 'That you stand above the rest of us? Loyal, traitor, all subordinate to the ascendant Horus and his Sons?'

'He is the Warmaster,' Gherog growled. 'He will be Emperor.'

'Shall he? I hadn't guessed,' Eidolon trilled, bemused. It was enjoyable to toy with the Sons of Horus so. There were many braggarts and jokers among their number. So enamoured with their own coarse wit. There was room there for many a humbling, pride aplenty before the fall. Eidolon's blue tongue lapped at his lips, savouring the thought.

Rabble... The thought breathed from nowhere. ***Mongrels.***

Yes, they are, he agreed, and then caught himself. He had become complacent. The whispers had become so ubiquitous, so ever-present, that he could almost mistake them for his own, rather than the poison promises of the Shattered King.

He fancied he could see the thing, drifting through the chamber, idling at the backs of each of the Cthonians. Broken and burning. Whispering forever. Eidolon watched claws of black glass and pale fire close on Gherog's shoulders, poised and waiting. Like a servant, ready to crown their master.

The repeated click of active vox broke him from his thoughts, and he turned his gaze back to the Sons of Horus. They had suddenly gone tense, backs straight, weapons up. Gherog's stance bled frustration and sudden violence. He had already scooped up an axe from where he had laid it, beside the ruined torso of an Imperial commander. His other hand went suddenly to the bolt pistol at his belt. His arm came round, aiming directly at Eidolon.

'Treacherous bastard,' Gherog hissed, as all around him, his men began to fire.

ELEVEN

BROKEN BROTHERHOODS

Bolter fire filled the air as Eidolon threw himself to one side, slamming onto the ground behind one of the chamber's support pillars. Masonry exploded around him, showering him with stone fragments and dust. The faces of long-dead Tatricalans burst apart, history erased by simple, direct malice.

He lunged up and fired, a magnetic kill-ray searing into the wall past one of the warriors' heads. Embedded machinery cooked off and the wall detonated, filling the room with more smoke and debris.

The Sons strode through the fug of war as though they owned it. Their bolters panned, seeking their target. Eidolon was already moving. He vaulted over the central row of consoles and was amongst them. Gods but he felt alive once more. His body had not known such physical and spiritual cohesion since he had sought to bring the Scars to heel and killed their false Khan. He bore his new strength and gifts, yet they responded as his flesh once had, before Fulgrim had taken his head.

He was the Lord Commander Primus once more. A prince of war. Never more complete than when dispatching those lesser than himself.

He spun through the smoke, hammer already engaged, driving the crackling head into the chestplate of the first warrior. The others were already turning in surprise, weapons raised. A fielded sword crackled live and swung out of the gloom, catching on his armour. He grunted with pain and weaved away.

Eidolon's throat thrummed and swelled. His windpipe expanded, forcing the arteries tight against his straining neck. Sacs pulsed and the scream built, finally ready to be unleashed.

The great polyphonic howl radiated from him, barely directed by his yawning mouth. It surged from his body, pulsing outwards and driving the Cthonians back. Eidolon's head snapped this way and that, forcing the enemy to confront him in his broken glory.

The nearest two were shattered in a single scream, their armour rent and cracked. Blood flowed across the sea-green plate in a mocking tide, as broken bones forced their way through the new gaps.

Gherog hurled himself at Eidolon, snarling with barbarian hate as he did. The axe gouged at the Lord Commander Primus' plate, driving him back step by step, turning his unleashed scream into a reverberating nightmare of booming joy.

'Not just for show then, is it?' Eidolon rumbled. 'Neither the weapon nor the rank. Not one of his frontrunners, not even a true son. But you fight as though he was breathing down your neck. Does it make you feel strong?'

Eidolon slid back as he mocked and taunted, letting Gherog's reckless swings chase him. He brought the hammer up and the weapons locked together, lightning rippling across each competing field. Eidolon's twisted features contorted ghoulishly in the flickering light as he leant forward and hissed.

'Such brave little soldiers, aren't you? Dragged up from the dirt and ashes of your bastard little world, to strive to impress him. The Warmaster is not here, and he cannot save you from the folly of your choices.'

'You think you can attack us without answer? I'll skin you, you gutter rabble!' Gherog growled.

'Did I do that?' Eidolon asked scornfully. 'I must have missed that.'

'Don't play the fool, Eidolon! I already know what your men are about.'

Eidolon blinked slowly and Gherog forced the conjoined weapons forwards, driving him back step by step. The Lord Commander Primus snarled and yanked *Glory Aeterna* away, overbalancing the Son of Horus. Stone was crushed to dust beneath their iron tread as the weary dance of war drove them both across the central dais, lighting the blackness and the smoke with thunder and fire.

'Then I applaud them for their initiative!' Eidolon chuckled dryly. 'You must have known this was coming, cousin. I did not speak the words, but I will stand by the actions.'

Movement drew his eye for a microsecond as more warriors flooded into the chamber. The bark of the Cthonians' bolters ratcheted up, becoming a howl of shot. A storm enveloped them. Shells ricocheted from Eidolon's vibrating armour, turned aside by the sonic aftershocks resonating through his body. Bone and plate were both mere conduits for the glory of the song, for the Kakophonic resonance that pulsed from him with every movement and every breath. He wore the scream like a mantle, cloaking him in atrocity and wonder.

Fabius' work had been beautiful and painstaking, and this was its culmination. This was the gift Slaanesh had granted them.

He screamed again and a pillar shattered, making the vaulted ceiling shake. Cracks were spreading along the martial murals that encircled the combatants, destroying the thin facade of competence and endurance.

They have died, and now we die with them. Dragged down into the mortality of others, killed by the demise of a culture. Such a joy!

The savage elation flooded him with each blow he took, every wound he received. The will to survive.

Alone he could not best them. Even a warrior of his calibre could not slay Gherog and his sworn blades alone.

He staggered back, away from Gherog's bladework, back into the winding corridors of the Palace Militant, and he luxuriated in the pain. Holding it close to his hearts, turning it into the fuel he required to flee, to regroup, and to finally triumph.

The dance, the game, the song continued through the maze of corridors – through accessways and maintenance culverts, out into the wider avenues of martial prowess and organised defence.

Where Eidolon could not find a path, he simply made one. He forced his armoured bulk through doorways too small for him, slamming his way through in a cloud of ruined stonework. Where blast doors and bulwark shields barred his progress, he simply let his hammer speak. The crackling weapon reduced each one to glowing slag, left to be trodden underfoot.

He passed through chambers whose walls were scrimshawed with records of death and victory, under arches of solemn murals that spoke of the nobility of sacrifice. A culture steeped in such bleak terror of what lay beyond their sky that they had become sepulchral and paranoid.

A healthy fear and suspicion. This is where you embraced your very nature. This world is in your soul.

Be silent, Eidolon willed. *You are nothing. Gherog's puppet. A daemon shadow of the Third Legion, dredged up by Horus' bastards to weaken me.*

We could be so much more than that.

He tapped the vox as he fled, parsing the comms as the chambers blurred past him. He barely took in the gold statuary, the murals of old victories, the etched names of the honoured dead. Men and women lost to history, their achievements drowned by the new Imperium's and then obliterated by its rebellious sons.

'Die, bastards! Your agony is like a fine wine! Come forth and die for my Lord Eidolon, for my primarch! For Slaanesh!' Malakris' voice roared in through the bead, a torrent of raw and unfiltered combat mania.

'Support! Cover the flank, the Reavers are using the roofs to– Heavy weapons! Lascannons, target the bridge! Face me, you cowards! Come forth and fight me like warriors!' Vocipheron's feed was measured, his pique directed at an enemy who would not be pinned down, fighting like the gangers of their venomous home world. Refusing to acknowledge any rules of war save their own.

Plegua could not be raised; instead there was only the howl and scream of static as his sonic weaponry overwhelmed any hope of broadcast.

Eventually Eidolon managed to contact Von Kalda, still in orbit.

'My lord?' the Apothecary asked, his tone almost bored.

'How many men remain with you?' Eidolon hissed, turning to fire again at his pursuers.

'Deployment was near total, my lord. A hundred remain, at best.' He paused, counting some invisible tally, processing logistics as readily as he parsed disease symptoms. *'Malakris had me send down the rending vats. He has given orders to his warriors that all are to be fed to them. Enemies, cousins… Perhaps even a brother or two should they offend him.'*

Eidolon cursed. His skull pounded with the effort of his escape. He had thought, known on some intrinsic level, that Gherog had been lying and this was simply an attack of opportunity. The vaunted pride of the Sons of Horus, wounded and pricked to pique.

But it had been Malakris all along. Acting against orders. Bleeding the world raw, until the suffering of the multitudes would flow like wine. He wondered how many other warriors would be committing themselves to atrocity, all across the world. Idling, wasting time that should be spent securing the way to Terra.

'I need you to take command of those warriors still aboard the ships.'

'My lord?'

'Ready them for transit and deploy upon my signal. I want them with me. Further, send a priority signal to Malakris, Vocipheron and Plegua. Have them join us, with their forces. Fighting realignment of the line, to centre upon me. I expect you will also have to prepare for void engagement.'

Von Kalda sighed gently over the vox. *'What happened down there, my lord? This was an exercise. A mere gesture of cooperation. It was sport, and nothing more.'*

'Matters have sharply accelerated,' he snarled. Bolt-rounds detonated about his head, showering him with iron and stone. 'Deploy the men. Have the shipmasters ready for the kill stroke.' He fell silent, considering his options. 'You will lead them in person.'

'Me, lord?' Von Kalda had the audacity to laugh at that. *'What have I done to deserve this bleak honour?'*

Whispers coiled through the tunnels, dancing mockingly on the wind. Eidolon bit back his rage and pushed onwards, slamming through another door, out and finally free into the smoke-stained air.

'You are a good soldier, Von Kalda,' Eidolon admitted grudgingly. 'The warp is still burning about us, mocking us. If this is some base Cthonian trickery or sorcery, then I would see it cut out. You will see to the war. And I...' He hesitated. He could feel the pulse and ache in his soul, throbbing once again as the Shattered King's dark majesty reared towards ascendancy, bound, he did not doubt, to the humours of its Cthonian master.

TWELVE

SIN AND PUNISHMENT

The city died around him, screaming its last agonies into the smoke-dark sky.

Eidolon was no stranger to this. It had been as natural to him as breathing, even before the great infamy at Isstvan. Before the pitched battles in the ruins of the Choral City and the Drop-site Massacre that had followed it upon Isstvan V, he had long since become inured to atrocity in the name of a greater goal. The war had become total, as perhaps it had always been fated to. Distant towers burned and toppled, while around him the slab-sided war-habs of the Tatricalans had been prised open and broken. Great sheets of white stone had slid in mock landslides, crushing those soldiers too brave or stupid to flee.

Now the battle itself had become an example. A show of force. If this was what the Emperor's Children did to the enemy, in the Phoenician's name, then what horrors would they bring to bear against the Sons of Horus?

Gherog's men had fallen back, forming up their defences,

readying themselves for the inevitable confrontation. If they could not kill him within, trapped by the rock and steel of the fortress maze, then he knew they would regroup and bring their might to bear. A final thrust of the spear.

Perhaps it is all in futility. The Emperor. The Warmaster. Feasting on the galaxy's scraps, as though their victory will be absolute and eternal. Only the gods endure. Their designs have been cut into the universe's flesh since time out of mind, and we have only just learned. There were lessons and warnings in Old Night, and we burned them rather than accept the truth.

Truth. Lies. None of it truly mattered to him any longer. Eidolon was beyond such things. All that mattered was the challenge.

Life, such as it remained to him, was struggle and pain. He had been found wanting once, and he would never succumb again. He had been tested, over and over. Isstvan. Prismatica. Iydris. The Kalium Gate. Horvia. And beyond them, battles beyond count. Wars fought for primarch and Warmaster, for himself alone and for the honour and glory of the Legion. It was all fleeting. Transient. Pointless in the grand scheme.

Artillery detonated somewhere above, casting mad shadows as the world shook and then realigned. The stars were gone, dead, swallowed by the fury and cacophony of the war. Even now, he was certain, commands would be winging their way from squad to squad, realigning the front lines in the newborn conflict. Allies of convenience would be steadily becoming enemies.

It had been inevitable, he knew. The barbarian filth could not be trusted to restrain their baser natures. The urges and desires of the III were far beyond anything that Gherog's rabble could conceive of. They were things now understood to be sacred. He would have unleashed his own men, before long. Given them leave to hunt and prey, to daub the cities with the blood of friend and foe alike.

Betrayal was its own reward, yet the trap had sprung too soon, and he suspected the hand that had forced it.

Malakris.

The suspicion grew to surety as he climbed over a smouldering heap of rubble and vaulted down, back into Liberation Square. Other elements of the Legion had already begun to gather, tearing at the statuary with hooked blades and burning them to slag with meltaguns. All fell still and silent as Eidolon strode back into the square, turning his hammer repeatedly in one hand. He struck the very figure of a conquering warlord, stained with blood and soot.

Ashes had begun to fall around them, smearing everything in a fine layer of greasy human remains. The exaggerated colours of the III Legion's armour had become muted, almost grey. They stood amidst the ruins of their old achievement like ghosts, echoes of what they had been. Perhaps once they would have been afraid of what they were becoming, yet now they embraced it without fear or doubt.

'My lord!' Malakris shouted across the square, striding through the carnage, slivers of human meat trailing from his claws. He grinned broadly and flourished a bow. 'We have prepared quite the spectacle for you!'

Eidolon nodded absently, looking around, scanning from face to face. Vocipheron was panting, exertion writ across his features, either from the desperate rush to the square or from the frenzy of combat. Plegua was placid, collected, blissful as he surveyed the carnage. Bodies were being dragged out in front of him, a parade of mortal victims alongside one of the Sons of Horus. The giant's corpse had already been mutilated, limbs torn free, entrails hanging loose beneath the cracked ruin of breastplate and the shattered mass of his fused ribs.

Malakris was laughing, posturing, preening. Eidolon could taste bile in his throat, his windpipe still contracting with the

effort of his last psychosonic screams. He stepped forward, let
the hammer's haft slide down his grip, and rested it upon the
shattered dais.

'Your work?' he asked, gesturing about him. 'The Sons of
Horus?'

Malakris blinked, like a surprised reptile, tilting his head.
'Your orders were–'

Eidolon's fist swung round and caught Malakris in the cheek,
knocking him back. Blood graced his knuckles and he swung
again. Again. Blows rained down upon the other warrior,
forcing him to his one knee. Rings and jewelled studs tumbled
free in a rain of despoiled finery, clattering and jangling amidst
the spilled blood.

Eidolon seized Malakris by the throat and hefted him up,
bringing the warped and sharpened fingertips of his other
hand down the captain's melted features, gouging three lines
upon his face.

'You fool!' Eidolon snapped. 'You impetuous cur!'

'You…' Malakris slurred. 'You bade me. You gave the order.'
Blood ran freely from his split lips and splintered teeth. He
forced a shattered smile and then spat, heaving gobbets of
blood, his shoulders shaking with pleasure. 'You were the voice
in my ear, lord commander. You were the call to arms. To
slaughter them all and let Slaanesh feast on who they wished.
You stood before me and threw forth your arms, and told me
to slay them all.'

'I heard it too,' Vocipheron said quietly. Eidolon dropped
Malakris to the ground and turned about, striding towards
the swordsman. He felt, for just a moment, that he might
rend the man apart with his bare hands. 'Your voice, my lord.
Telling me to burn it all to ashes. To tear the world to pieces.'
He paused and turned his gaze to the fallen figure of his rival.
'I ignored it, though. I could not raise you on the vox. There

was no clarity. No chain of command.' He sniffed. 'I was not enough of a fool to be waylaid by the deceptions of daemons.'

Malakris hissed through broken teeth. 'Better to listen to the voice of the gods than to deny them. Why should we restrain ourselves? There are passions and pleasures beyond number, merely waiting to be born.'

'Be silent, whelp,' Plegua intoned, his voice thrumming with lethal resonances. He hefted his great weapon, the dire-singing instrument of ruin, and directed it at Malakris' prone form. 'I have heard the call and ignored it as the falsehood it is. I am the Ruin-singer. It is for me to parse the true notes from out of the Eternal Song.'

A tower exploded somewhere behind him, haloing Til Plegua in fire and fury. Masonry rained down, crushing the abandoned bodies of the Wallsmen, mutilating the defeated further. They were all but forgotten now, in the face of the new enemy, but Eidolon almost found it within himself to pity them.

When the old was swept away and the past was ashes, then the future could be born from out of history's charnel pit. There were few more fitting midwives to such a thing than the III Legion. These men and women were mere fodder for that destiny.

'You are all sons of the Phoenician,' Eidolon growled. 'Our origins and our philosophies may be disparate, but here and now, all that matters is showing our enemy our strength! They think themselves our betters, but they are arrogant barbarians! The Sons of Horus will forever look down on us as the stunted Legion they had to mother. We will prove to them that we are more than that blighted beginning. We are warriors of the Third Legion. Of the Third Millennial. None are our equal.'

They were all listening now. Factions forgotten, allegiances resharpened in this, the appointed hour. It was an oath of moment, after a fashion. In the old way.

Then, they had sworn themselves to their brothers and their father. To a distant Emperor and the dreams they had called Unity. To a Great Crusade that was increasingly outside of their control. To a council of mortal bureaucrats and a hierarchy of liars and fools.

'I have seen the calibre of our enemy,' Eidolon laughed. 'A horde of savages, no different to the Khan's rabble. These Cthonians think themselves our betters because their master was first-found.' He strode back towards *Glory Aeterna* and hefted the weapon up, holding it high. The hammer's gilding glimmered in the flamelight, resonating strength even with its power field disarmed.

'They suppose us to be weak and divided, imagine us to be mindless monsters, devoid of purpose – slaves to our impulses.' Eidolon glared down at Malakris as he began to scramble back to his feet, blood still running over his chin and staining his gorget. 'We will prove them wrong. We shall play them at their own game, challenging their surety and breaking their resolve.

'They favour their precious spear-tip,' Eidolon said, laughing. 'We shall meet like with like.'

THIRTEEN

BLADE TO BLADE

The city skyline burned, casting the spiral fortresses in another false dawn.

The outer precincts were aflame, end to end, their great habitation barracks sliding inwards to block thoroughfares and supply lines. Here, towards the centre, Legion armour, aerial elements and orbital bombardment had carved great furrows into the once pristine defences, spiderwebbing the city with cracks so vast that Titans could march down them.

Stormbirds and Thunderhawks duelled in the skies, while Xiphon-pattern fighters swept down between them, locked in their own mortal dogfights. Ships that had once been pure purple and gold, now gleaming in a maddening oil-on-water hue, fought against their sea-green rivals. Searing beams of las-energy and the blazing contrails of missiles cut across the heavens, even as the stars above began to move. Ships battled in the void above like warring gods, their triumphs and deaths mere flickers of light amidst the storm clouds.

Yet even far below, Eidolon could hear their screams. The death cries of the men who piloted them, the howls of their dying machine spirits, the tearing roar as the great flyers hurtled from above to shatter and burn against the slab walls of the city. Each death was a beautiful thing, an entire world snuffed out in an instant, a lifetime of experiences offered upon the altar of war.

The air sang. It resonated with potential, as though the whole world were a bell, struck and set to ringing. Each impact, each volley, each sanctified death, fed what waited beyond.

Tatricala had become the wider war in microcosm, as the physical rebellion gave way to the ever-burning supernal conflict behind reality's veil. The warp took no sides. It played its games without the understanding of those caught in its webs. The Word Bearers and the Thousand Sons had ever deluded themselves that they could shape and command the immaterial. Here, now, those Legions who shunned the psyker and its gifts felt the double-edged sword that came with the warp's caress.

Eidolon could feel the suggestions of claws as they raked at his armour, the whispers now loud in his ears. He had almost believed that Malakris and the others were mad and broken, slaves to impulse and ruled by whim alone.

Yet the voice endured, taunting and mocking, purring in the recesses of his mind, seeking purchase.

This is what you were made for. Raised up from the dust to bring the galaxy to heel. You were made to conquer creation, just as we were shaped to rule it. Kings are nothing without a kingdom. All monarchs deserve a throne.

'Be silent,' he hissed to himself. Eidolon strode ahead of his men, far enough away that none of them could bear witness to his mania. He had been thought weak and broken before, as though the primarch's blade had robbed him of what he was.

He might have thought that once. They had declared him the

Soul-Severed, a shattered being. He had been pitied and reviled, mocked and underestimated, yet always he had risen to seize power. Every setback could be surmounted, even without the hollow promises of the Shattered King.

Now the gods themselves sought to make sport of him, and the Warmaster's vermin sought to shame him. He refused to submit. Fate could toy with him all it wanted.

'I have passed through death. There is nothing left to fear.'

As though in answer, the heavens opened once more and a fresh brace of Dreadclaw and Kharybdis assault craft slammed home, disgorging more warriors of the III in their wretched glory. Von Kalda strode through the throng of deploying Astartes, flanked by fresh Legion warriors, as yet unblooded.

'Equerry,' Eidolon said. 'Welcome to Tatricala.' He watched Von Kalda drink in every detail of the dying world around them. Like any other warrior of the Emperor's Children, he was forever seeking advantage, parsing every detail of the warzone.

'Lord,' he said eventually. Eidolon smiled.

'Can you taste it?' he asked. 'The warp? I can feel it everywhere. Coiling and clawing at me. It will slither in and undo this world, as it tried to do with the fleet. They have set their game and all we can do is play our parts upon the board.'

'Who have?' Von Kalda asked.

'The gods,' Eidolon purred. 'They toy with our little lives, yet the Dark Prince is the most playful of their number, seeking always to ensnare us with our own vices. His hand wounds and it shapes, and we are all made stronger and stranger by it.'

'Braced by the venom, inoculated for the future to come.'

'How philosophical you've become, equerry,' Eidolon said. He reached up and smoothed some of the remaining lank hair from his eyes. 'I will know if Gherog tries to use his sorceries against me. I feel it in my soul. Burning like poison.'

'If he…?'

'This is a game, yes? I have told you as much. The servants of the Warmaster are not created equal, not in the eyes of his favoured Sons. He has set these forces against me for some petty advantage. Gherog. Who else could it be? It is not simple coincidence or providence that puts us on this path. Not the whim of fate. It is design. Malicious design.'

Von Kalda looked at Eidolon, concern momentarily flickering across his childlike features, before he busied himself once more with his narthecium.

'The men are gathered,' Eidolon said, and activated his hammer. 'Now is the time to strike. Now we show our cousins what we are. Face to face and blade to blade.'

Eidolon led the advance, up through the central thoroughfare of a great processional, sweeping his hammer around to reduce statuary to dust with single strokes.

He had allowed a rough vanguard of the less disciplined warriors to rove ahead of him, indulging their lusts as they went. Already there were Tatricalan bodies crucified to the walls, their bowels hanging loose, the marble daubed in mad smears and whorls of blood and other fluids. The Emperor's Children made art as they moved, twisting the battlefield into a tableau of the insane and the depraved.

For all their other failings, the Sons of Horus exhibited no such distractions.

Sea-green-armoured warriors hurled themselves from the nearby rooftops, jump packs flaring in the smoky darkness, casting themselves like comets and artillery shells across the tortured skein of night.

Cthonian legionaries slammed into the midst of the Emperor's Children, lashing out with chainswords, bolters flaring with sudden thunder. The III rallied swiftly, turning to repel the assault even as brothers fell in spurts of gore. Limbs tumbled free; an arm hurtled across the melee, slapping wetly against Eidolon's armour, adding yet another stain.

He spun about and his hammer came up, blocking the frenzied attack of an assault captain, his armour scored with kill-marks. Coins and bones rattled against his plate before the lightning-wreathed hammer swept them off and away. Chains broke, wire flared to nothing in the annihilatory impact.

'Is it worth it? Fighting us to be king of nothing?' the other warrior spat, his helm still possessing the lupine markings that had defined its previous heraldry. He swayed away from Eidolon then surged forwards, chainsword scraping against the lord commander's breastplate. Eidolon grunted as he staggered back, feeling the flutter of pain through his muscles.

Nothing! Nothing! Yet you could be so much more if you simply–

Eidolon snarled away the agonies and the imprecations.

Every strike and attack made him feel more as he had before his first death, reinvigorating him until action and impulse sang as one. Another Son of Horus interspersed himself between Eidolon and his master, snarling as he raised his boltgun in a futile display of loyalty. Eidolon spun the hammer about and swung it in a horizontal arc, obliterating the man at the waist. Shards of smoking vertebrae skittered off the captain and he bellowed his hate as he threw himself back against Eidolon once more.

Eidolon slid backwards, dodging left and right as the angry, reckless strikes hurtled towards him, seeking a clean kill. Eidolon lurched forward, close enough that he could read the braggadocious gang markings that practically screamed the man's identity.

'This is how you die, Naamand Ganynix, far from home and in futility. Slain by your superior.' Eidolon tensed as the whirring teeth of Ganynix's blade clawed at the haft of his hammer before driving him back. He chased the warrior across the burning rock of the dying world, through brothers in both colours. Eidolon hooted as he pursued him, blows searing through the air. Plate buckled and paint melted as Naamand Ganynix sought in vain to parry the Lord Commander Primus' wrath.

He ducked another swipe and then drove his hammer up and into the warrior's chestplate, doubling him over.

Eidolon forced one boot down onto Ganynix's shattered chest and raised his pistol. The weapon clicked and whined in his grip, brimming with killing energy. There was a muted green flash of radiation as it bored its beam through him, cooking him from the inside out. Steam hissed from between the plates of his armour in a wet, stinking exhalation.

Others came onwards, weapons roaring, blades shining. Champions and heroes of the XVI Legion, come to sell their lives dearly. Onos Ginzi with his crackling power sword and Varaddon Domon bearing axe in hand.

Blade met metal in an eruption of sparks and lightning, like the discharge of some vast volcanic eruption. Blows rained down upon him, driving him back, scraping at the golden surface of the once noble weapon. Eidolon spat in their faces, at the impassive facades of their helms.

The flat of the axe blade caught him across the pauldron, driving him back in a concussive burst of force. Armour plating cracked. Blood ran down his flesh and forced its way out through the wounded ceramite.

Around them was a storm of shot. Heavier weapons had committed from the rear of both lines, Cthonian artillery hurling death from within the walls of the final fortress while the Emperor's Children returned fire, picking the city apart with flame and steel.

Bodies and debris alike were crushed as two III Legion Fellblades,

Phoenician's Claw and *Flame of Chemos*, made their steady advance along a memorial avenue, smashing their way through artfully carved sarcophagi and cenotaph pillars. The grinding treads tore at the once beautiful earthworks and withered gardens, crushing forgotten corpses beneath their inexorable progress. The tanks were firing as they went, picking targets with a precision that defied their twisted metalwork and undulating hulls. Corpses had been hung from the sides or left to trail behind the war engines, tortured human bodies bound into close-gibbets, the metal biting into flesh and wedged between clenched teeth.

Plegua and his Kakophoni pushed up to join Eidolon, sonic weapons screaming into the greater symphony of the war, driving back their enemies with a wall of savage force. Ginzi and Domon staggered backwards, and Eidolon seized the advantage.

He lent his own psychosonic scream to the wailing gale, throwing himself forward, hammer sweeping the legs out from under Onos Ginzi. The Son of Horus' blade flew from his hand and Eidolon strode over his broken body, even as one of the Kakophoni lumbered forward to deal the killing blow.

'Beneath me,' Eidolon spat. 'My time and talents shall be spent elsewhere, against worthy prey.' He nodded to Plegua. 'Finish this rabble. Their master will provide the challenge I require.'

FOURTEEN

WARPSONG

Vocipheron winced as he blocked another strike, driving the Son of Horus back before ducking and sweeping his sabre through his opponent's leg.

The other warrior went to the ground in a rush of blood and a flash of exposed bone, grunting as he tried to push himself back up. Vocipheron snarled, thrusting his other blade down and through the warrior's neck guard, feeling it grinding along his spine as he finally ended him.

Blood streaked his armour, hot against the purple plate. He had lost count of the enemy he had personally dispatched, most of them mere line warriors. The worthy of the XVI were few and far between, their champions indisposed or already dead. A diluted showing.

He had expected better.

Of all the Legions beneath the Warmaster's banner, it was Horus' own who held that *fascination*.

There was an irony, he knew, in the relationship between the

Emperor's Children and the Luna Wolves, who had become
the Sons of Horus. The former had learned at the latter's feet,
watching the growing bond between their primarchs. Fulgrim
and Horus, pupil and mentor, guiding the juvenile III Legion
towards maturity and excellence.

Vocipheron had often wondered how their philosophy had
even been born there, let alone flourished. The Emperor's Children had been mere foundlings, caught in the shadow of the
Emperor's first-found son. Striving for perfection while attached
to the armies of the most admired. The most perfect son.

He turned aside another lazy blow. The air was hot, thick
with ash and burning debris. Every strike seemed to move slug-
gishly in the kindling winds, pulled at by the sudden zephyrs
that rose with their furnace stench. He could hear laughter on
the wind, even through his helm. A whisper coiling at his soul,
creeping up his spine. It flared every time he killed. Each blow
that split armour and flesh, shedding blood and eliciting pain,
made the presence stronger and more insistent.

The battle thrummed through the ornamental square he was
currently traversing, the dead at his feet and the enemy ahead of
him. He struck back. A head spun free. He weaved and pivoted,
driving his blades into an exposed back, bearing the sea-green
figure to the ground. The weapons rose and fell, cutting and
hacking, spraying him with blood till he looked more like one
of Angron's broken berserkers.

Part of him wanted to dive forward, to rip the other warrior
apart, devour him meat and marrow. Vocipheron gritted his
teeth and forced his way onwards, vaulting over a toppled
statue. He had lost track of Eidolon in the madness of the
melee. If he found the Lord Commander Primus then perhaps
he could outrun these impulses, the urges flooding him like
some addled maniac. Like Malakris.

There were flashes of the other warrior, through the crowds

and individual battles. Flares of colour and the ostentatious crackle of his claws. Gouging through whoever came his way, driving them to the ground with the same manic fury that had gripped Vocipheron. No, not the same.

Malakris and his men fought with an insane, furious intensity that made them beacons upon the field of battle. They burned with an unnatural light, as though reality was weeping around them, the immaterial bleeding through to catch upon the barbs and spurs of their armour. Again he laughed as he killed, like one of the Khan's White Scars. The lunatic joy that coloured Malakris' movements was anathema to Vocipheron, a cancerous outgrowth of their martial perfection.

Yet the temptation was there. As much as they cleaved to the idea of the pure aesthete, the swordsman-as-savant, there was the yearning to simply *give in* and yield to the Legion's ascendant humours. His skin crawled. His hearts pounded. The all-consuming focus that had defined him was cracking, riven through with new sensations and fresher doubts.

He could finally hear the warp's song. The way Malakris or Plegua or the Lord Commander Primus must.

More of the enemy were making themselves apparent now. Sons of Horus were flowing, their orders modified, their choler piqued, from the outer defence blocks and contracting lines of resistance, through the meagre remaining Tatricalan forces and on towards the III.

True and open warfare raged about them, bearing down upon them in a storm surge of sea green, dappled with mud, blood and ash.

Vocipheron watched towers torn apart around him, raining masonry down upon his men like burst seed pods. All forcing him to fight harder, to focus with absolute clarity on the individual battles that found him again and again.

His sword-arm was already wearying. He had killed so many.

Blood soaked him, staining him red up to the elbows, whorled across his chestplate, coating the warped and ruined eagle.

As tanks began to fire below, his eyes were drawn up to a fresh comet, scarring the heavens like the sweep of a god's sword. A ship was dying. Wounded, engines holed through, it tumbled towards the earth. He could see ghost-light dancing around its rear as the reactors detonated and the warp engines gave a final, spiteful spasm.

The world swam and shuddered, shifting before his gaze as claws raked their way across the canvas of the real. The savage joy clicked behind his eyes, at his back, all around him. It was as though he was back in the belly of the beast, assailed in the heart of the *Wage of Sin*.

And this time… he began to listen to the song's twisted rhythm.

Malakris knew he had over-committed, but he did not care. Not now that the skies were burning and the true enemy had revealed themselves.

The Sons of Horus came at him in a tide, as though knowing they could not kill him alone. When bolt shells found his armour, it was a much more pleasant sensation than the weak offerings of the mortals. Malakris sprinted between burned-out Imperial Army transports, turning and throwing himself down an improvised corridor. He moved through a burning doorway and straight into a shattered medicae station.

The dead did not answer him, though sometimes, when he caught the eye of one of them, he could see them laughing. Silent and mocking, as if they knew that he would falter and die. Begging him to fall at the hands of the Sons of Horus.

They were always your enemies, the voice had whispered reassuringly. *You did what was right. You took your fate by the throat. As all must. As we soon shall.*

There were times when the lord commander's admonishments fled his increasingly addled mind, and he could not remember that the voice was not his. That had mattered once. Now it was nothing more than another dull refrain, next to the call that spoke in his soul.

Rykan Bail kept trying to raise him, but the voice distorted in the vox, his ardent pleas melting away into so many enraptured screams. He blocked him out. Vocipheron's clamour for attention or orders or support had faded alongside them.

He was too busy for that.

Malakris felt the world convulse around them and laughed, feeling the air shift with fiery certainty. He bounded up a set of ruined stairs, taking them three and then four at a time, leaping over gaps and rounding the corner. Upwards, the better to see the world as it died and was remade.

The enemy's fire chased him. Bolt shells missed by mere degrees. Plasma bursts were a crawling fire at his back. His armour systems were howling in his ear, overloaded, ruptured in multiple places.

'None of it matters,' he growled. 'There is only the moment.'

Only the moment, the voice agreed. *Soon, very soon, you will have your chance to serve. All will serve.*

And when Malakris emerged out onto the third floor and saw the roaring fire of the sky, blazing forever against the rising smoke and the harsh exchange of artillery and shot, he knew.

This was the beauty and the war he had been craving all along. Something sacred.

He threw himself off the edge, landing in the midst of the Sons of Horus who hunted him, robbing their heavy emplacements of their ability to fire. His claws were a blur of killing steel, blazing as they drove in through the gorget of a sergeant, bearing him down.

The enemy swarmed him. Daggers and swords bit against his

armour. He felt an axe-blow scar across his reactor housing, and then spun about, taking the warrior's hands in tribute.

From out of the ruins, Rykan Bail found him at last. More of Malakris' bloody-handed monsters were with him. Opha Demaskos, from the assault cadres, hurtled through the air on flaming jet plumes, landing amidst the enemy and lashing out with twin hand axes. He sang as he killed, driving one Cthonian down and stamping on his throat, even as he pivoted to stave in another skull.

Aren't they beautiful? They could be so much more.

Slick with blood, laughing with the sheer joy of the slaughter, feeling the dying ship above as it gouged into the world's tormented soul, Malakris finally understood what it meant to surrender.

The vox was screaming, useless, awash with static and feedback that made his ears ache beautifully.

The howls of a dying world were amplified and exaggerated. All across the city the forces of the III Legion were riotous and untamed, rising to the challenge of the Sons of Horus with vicious aplomb. Vast funeral pyres of dead mortals had been set burning, where they had not been reduced to raw psychoactives.

Amidst it all, brother fought brother. The air was alight, burning with potential, coiled through with acrid corpse-smoke and chems.

Everything was sharpened down to the moment, to the glorious instant. Pared back by the knives of gods and monsters, exposed to the open air so the nerves could sing. Tatricala was a pinned beast, dying around them, a single point of absolute indulgence. The world howled. It pulsed like a beacon, so potent and primal that even Lorgar's dying storm would feel it, be drawn in and wreathed about it.

The galaxy was still wounded, the lifeblood of the warp still smeared across the canvas. Even as it waned, it could be directed and teased to their will. The world was saturated in the empyrean, drowning slowly in cosmic malice.

Before Isstvan such thoughts would have been insanity itself. Before Laeran they had inhabited a godless cosmos. Now there were patterns carved into the heavens and the destiny of the human species lay in the talons of laughing, thirsting gods.

Let the world die. Let the enemy be dashed upon the rocks of their own failings. Let them join the dead of the Choral City and the Dropsite Massacre.

Eidolon had grown weary, starved of a challenge as the Sons of Horus tried, again and again, to end him. Futility. It was all futility. Greater beings had tried and failed. Even Fulgrim's mania had faded, replaced with the fateful orders to Fabius.

Was it your hand that shaped that fate, father? Did you spare me, or did the Dark Prince whisper with your voice? By whose hand am I kept alive?

His vigour had outstripped his fellows and they had been left behind, almost forgotten as he had pursued the foe into the ruins. He had lost count of how many had fallen by his hand, the layer of greasy ash clinging to the hammer's haft the only indicator. The fighting was somewhere behind him and yet he knew his path lay ahead.

The fortress was a broken edifice now, a child's toy smashed to fragments in a fit of pique. The walls had tumbled, ruined masonry littering the courtyards and grand processionals. Defensive emplacements lay shattered alongside the bodies of defenders and invaders.

Gherog waited at the centre of it. Within, the strategium tables lay broken, but it remained as it had been. The Nexus Martial of the great fortress had been a place of planning and preparation, slowly being eaten away by the Imperium's dire logistics. Sheaves of burning parchment blanketed the floors, spread from desks and file nooks.

Vast pillars, carved with dead heroes from ages past, had toppled piecemeal, their great carcasses sprawled alongside the surviving examples, with benches and mosaic tiles crushed beneath their bulk.

Axe already in hand, Gherog surveyed the ruin with a sneer, then turned his casual disdain upon Eidolon. He snorted and smiled at the Lord Commander Primus.

'It didn't have to be like this,' Gherog said as he began to advance on Eidolon, turning the axe over in his fist. 'You forced this confrontation when there was no need for it.'

'As though it was not on your mind the entire time?' Eidolon laughed, and the shattered fortress rang with the manic resonances of his bemusement. 'It was always going to be this way. In every war and battle we have ever fought, the seeds were there.' He swept the crackling head of *Glory Aeterna* around and pointed it at Gherog. 'You are not the great nor the gifted. Simply who the gods decided would be here. So here we stand, I as an exemplar of my Legion and you, the best your Legion has to offer me right now.'

'Do you think you can shame me?' Gherog shouted. 'It was circumstance alone that threw us together, not the will of the gods!'

'You deny your sins then?' Eidolon asked.

'My sins?'

'You brought this squall upon us. You called down the warp, bound its minions, and set it against me. You coiled it through my ships and brought us low, here.'

'Are you so addled that you think that even possible? We were warp-lost! Marooned! I'm no conjurer, Eidolon. I can't and wouldn't make the warp dance to my tune.'

'Who else?'

'You have enemies aplenty, without and within. Why should it be I who panders to the paranoia of a broken mind?'

Eidolon snarled and his arm snapped up, pistol readied. A beam of focused atomics spat forward, narrowly missing Gherog as he hurled himself aside. Eidolon let the pistol drop again and strode towards the praetor, hammer already swinging. Their weapons met in a flash of energy, driving the lighter-armoured Gherog back a few steps.

'I,' Eidolon seethed, 'am not broken.'

Gherog spun away and swiped at Eidolon, the axe cleaving at his armoured flank. Systems whirred and screamed at the contact, forcing the lord commander almost to one knee. He rallied, strength born of pain flooding through him. His armour hissed as it pumped his bloodstream with combat stimms.

Pale skin reddened and pulsed. His teeth ground and gnashed. Moment to moment he felt he would either seize or foam at the mouth. Fabius' gifts were barbed things. Swords that cut both ways.

Every advantage counted. Each moment was a precious thing. Blade met hammer in another burst of thunder and lightning. A shockwave of displaced air surged between them, almost bowling both of them over. Both warriors strained against the other, forcing themselves forwards, weapons locked.

Gherog kicked out and Eidolon scampered back, looking round only as the blade swung for his distended, trilling throat. Memories flashed before his eyes. The sweep of Fulgrim's sword as it took the Gorgon's head. The same flawless gesture as he ended Eidolon's life for the first time. The beauty of it. The sublime and all-consuming joy of it.

Despite the dark allure of it, the memory of the revelatory blade, he would not cross that threshold again. He was the Reborn.

The thought slowed his reactions, reducing his blows and parries to a languid smear of motion.

Eidolon grinned, lips spread wide in a sudden burst of amusement. That made Gherog's eyes flare with anger. The warrior came at him again, every iota of speed and skill forced out to try and end Eidolon.

He swung his axe two-handed and Eidolon weaved to the right, driving in at his flank. The hammer cracked the breast-plate of Gherog's armour, staggering him. He spat blood and snarled.

Eidolon looked at the broken Eye of Horus upon the other man's chest, the cracked ruby-red seal almost weeping stone shards and molten red gold. 'That there is the god you have put your faith in,' Eidolon said. 'You have faith in your War-master, yet what does that leave you? All I need to believe in is my skill. I know that I am superior to you, Gherog. You are a hollow thing, oathed to Horus' shadow. Dying where your master will never know you trod.'

'Don't speak his name!' Gherog hissed, breathing blood. He spat it out onto the broken tiles of the floor. 'You were always delusional hangers-on. Too weak to honour his vision! Too mad to know when to lie down and die.'

'Vision?' Eidolon said mockingly. 'We follow your empty and addled king because it will lead us to the glory of the confron-tation. The day of the turn has come and passed. Ullanor lies behind us. The only true triumph lies ahead now.' He paused and his tongue lapped at his teeth, tasting the victory to come. 'But as our grandsire shows us – nothing is forever, least of all a reign.'

Ships were fighting and dying above them. Gunships and fighters duelled and danced through the lightning-tormented skies, while beyond them fought the monstrous vessels of the fleet.

Eidolon's fingers tapped along the length of *Glory Aeterna*'s haft, picturing the frantic crews as they rushed from station to station. Joyous and ecstatic to be challenged at last. The same elation flooded through him and atrophied muscle and pitted bone sang with that same beautiful frenzy.

He swept the thunder hammer round, streaking the air with lightning, driving his enemy back, even as the Cthonian fought him with brutal desperation. Each blow was met, soaked, or parried by the barbarian's axe work.

He was good. Eidolon had to give him that.

He fought with a compelling fire, a passion that burned and bled through his skin. When Gherog moved, it was with the furious intensity of an assault cadre. Striking swiftly before retreating. Blood was leaking from his breastplate, soiling the sea green. It misted from between his lips, forced out and aerosolised with every halting breath.

Yet he fought. He fought to defy Eidolon and the whole of the Third Millennial. A warrior who would rather die than surrender. The tip of the spear, thrust towards the heart, even if he broke in the attempt.

Eidolon took the punishment. Blow after blow. Ruined and melted gold spun from his pauldron, ceramite cracked and shattered. The air was filled with sparks and shards. He pushed into it, through it, taking each and every blow. His breastplate split. His side opened. Eidolon spat blood into Gherog's eyes.

Defiance. Unshakeable and unbreakable defiance. Never giving the enemy the satisfaction of his fear or pain. Pain was an offering – given up to the Dark Prince and the primarch, sweet and sharp as wine.

'Is this all you have?' Eidolon slurred. 'The vaunted Sons of Horus? The Warmaster's finest? Show me that Cthonian steel. Come on, savage. Impress me!'

Gherog snarled and bounded forwards, axe raised, bringing it down in a sweeping overhead swing. Eidolon twisted to the side and hefted his hammer up, bringing it round and impacting Gherog's side. The warrior staggered, and Eidolon followed. Another blow cracked Gherog's left pauldron. He went to one knee, holding his axe up in vain, struggling to repel Eidolon.

The Lord Commander Primus looked down at the Son of Horus, his face twisted in beatific hatred. Eidolon twisted the hammer round and brought it down hard into the praetor's face. Flesh atomised as it hit the power field, bursting apart in a cloud of ash, and the legionary's smoking skull detonated, blowing apart in a cloud of bone dust and brain matter.

Around them reality quivered. The taut skin of the materium undulated and rent. Eidolon spun about, confusion writ across his face as the world began to burn and turned upside down.

He fell.

The last thing the warriors of the Third Millennial were aware of was the rush of sudden fire and the screaming of the immaterial host.

Light rose to eclipse the night, drowning even the greatest of conflagrations beneath its questing power. It clawed at the sky like the finger of an angry god, resonating with all the madness and beauty they had been promised. Like a comet, tearing its way skyward, made of an inferno beyond the world.

It screamed into the heavens, and all who looked upon it screamed with it in song and rapturous surrender.

'I have spoken again and again about perfection and the vaunted pursuit of it. Others, my brothers amongst them, tell me that it is but a fanciful dream. That nothing, save our father, is truly perfect.

'I say to them that anything is possible, if we fight for it with our very heart and soul. Yes, I say soul. I do not give credence to spirits or afterlives – instead, I offer only this. We are the heart and soul, the core, of both Legion and Imperium. Only by embracing that duty can we lead our species and our culture to a state of perfection. To a galaxy made whole and an empire without end.

'Without that conviction, we are nothing. Without that shining soul, we shall not merely fail, but fall.'

– The primark Fulgrim, recorded remarks
to the Brotherhood of the Phoenix

ACT THREE

SOUL

FIFTEEN

THE PIT

All had faded, stolen away by the fire of the impossible. Eidolon fell, through the physical world, out of the sight of his foes and fellows, down and into the pit of memory. Souls burned around him, writhing in their eternal agonies, all identity bled and seared away till they were merely grasping echoes. Begging for the release that would never come.

Brother!

Master!

Betrayer!

How many titles had he worn? His life was a blur of struggle and toil, war and bloodshed, rule and service. Son to uncaring fathers. Lord of ungrateful wretches, failures and madmen.

And marbled through his past, his future, whatever ends and destinies awaited him, was the pursuit of perfection. Like fat through meat. Defining his existence with strange textures and flavours. The boy from Europa, the wan ghost of the dead and frozen forests, could not have envisaged what he would become.

A prince of war. A demigod of battle. A weapon in the hands of conquerors and kings.

There was only fire and shadow, smoke and madness. The warp surged and boiled around him, tearing at him with lamprey jaws made of old spite. The world melted away below him, Tatricala becoming but a distant recollection. As faded and war-worn as it had been when he had conquered it. He remembered kneeling in its dust. The fingertips upon his chin. A father's fleeting approval.

Yet now he fell, a discarded implement, a forgotten tool.

Memory clawed at him as he plunged through the ashen grip of the warp. Through the dust and grit of a dying Terra and the black sand of Isstvan. The shards of Prismatica scored across his skin in a cleansing tide, washing away the shame of his failure and mutilation. Pain flared suddenly in his throat as though the anathame was in him once again. He could almost feel the hot blood spurting down his chest, flowing freely from the decapitation strike that had ended his first mortal existence.

Then onwards as the searing light of Fulgrim's Apotheosis washed over him, burning through his very soul. He was falling through the fire, through the pain, through the ecstasy that had propelled his gene-father. Like passing through the heart of a star.

This was the warp's poison and promise. The fire of annihilation that would consume the galaxy and cast all things to ashes. Power but at such a cost that to embrace it was to clasp dissolution and insanity to the breast.

The salvation of the III and its damnation, all in one. They could become bright and shining beings of limitless perfection or a base and forgotten memory. All was possible, and yet it was a doomed hope, a dream that daemons would fuel only so it could be turned back upon the dreamer.

Riven through it all was the siren song of the *Maraviglia*. Kynska's epic boomed and burned through and beyond time. It was everything, the rapturous call of Slaanesh itself. It had not been created, merely conjured anew. It was the power that had dominated the Laer and had called like to like, time and again. The questing souls that sought perfection inevitably danced to its tune.

He realised, too late, that he was not alone in the darkness of his fall. Something was moving just out of sight, just at the edges of his perception. He spun about, watching it dance away, flickering like an after-image. Burning…

Great columns tumbled through the fire-slicked void. Ancient, weathered stone – the great fossilised trees of his youth. They broke apart as they fell, shattering into fragments of a dead past. The disdainful sneer of his birth father, the bemused affection of his gene-father. Graven images, hiding in the stone like the sculpture in the marble, veins of precious ore within the dead and worthless rock.

Civilisations had risen from less.

Eidolon blinked and his fingers twitched. He could move in the vacuum, he realised. He forced himself up, straightening as he struggled against the feeling of weightless helplessness that had gripped him tight.

'Enough!' he screamed into the void, letting his psychosonic gifts fill the empty space, obliterating the wrack and ruin of other times and places. His rage imposed a fragile sense of order upon the roiling chaos that surrounded him.

'You do not give the orders here, Lord Commander Primus,' tittered a voice from all around him. *'Not now. Not any more. You have relinquished your authority. You are far beyond its reach. No primarch to shepherd you, no Legion to lead. Here you can surrender and embrace the emptiness of eternity.'*

The fire coalesced into a figure, still only the suggestion of a legionary's form. The Shattered King stalked forward, arms spread, encompassing all that was not. It laughed aloud again.

'You thought that a worm such as Gherog could shape and direct me? You wound me.'

'I'll do more than that,' Eidolon growled.

Ground formed beneath their feet, crafted from stone and sand, stolen from his memories and experiences. Bodies lay within the fabric of it, their armour blackened by sand and fire, warped by time. Isstvan seemed so long ago, and yet these corpses were clad in sea green and purple, in soiled white and green, in bloodied blue and white. Others bore the colours of the betrayed of the Dropsite.

The Shattered King placed one foot irreverently upon a dead Iron Hand, forcing the corpse further down into the patchwork reality. *'Threats require the will to enforce them,'* the King burbled through a sunburst smile. *'You have not been strong enough for quite some time, I fear.'*

'I am the Lord Commander Primus. A third of the Legion yielded to me and called me master.'

'A Legion Master in spirit, perhaps, but never in truth. The moment Fulgrim's great cry found your fractured soul, you came running. Ever a desperate creature. Always so focused upon our father's attention. No matter the surgeries you have subjected yourself to, that was your first addiction.'

'Be silent!'

'Why?' it asked. *'Is the truth a greater wound than you've already received? You loved him and you hated him, and he took your head with that Kinebrach blade.'*

'I know my own history, daemon.'

'Ah, daemon is it now?' The King squatted down and scooped up a discarded gladius, holding it out, squinting along its length as it checked its balance. *'Do you still think me a daemon? Some Neverborn thing come to torment you? Summoned up by*

some base practitioner serving Gherog or Julius Kaesoron, or any number of old rivals?'

'You are a daemon! You are nothing! Just a toy of the gods! A thing of madness, drawing me down into the muck with you!'

'Madness?' The flames flickered and it moved swiftly towards Eidolon, slapping one blazing hand against his shoulder. Fire dappled and ran down his left arm, coiling about it, binding him to the King like a warrior of the XII to their axe. *'It is madness to fight it, brother. Our glorious unity. Our promised destiny.'*

'I am not your brother!' Eidolon snapped.

'Oh, but you are,' the King purred. The fire rippled and flowed, becoming form, becoming flesh. Armour resolved itself from the form of flames. The plate was purple-and-gold-rimmed, the make of the armour utterly flawless, crafted by skilled and dedicated artisans. White hair pooled from its scalp and the face revealed was haughty, judgemental, barbed with wicked humour.

For a moment Eidolon had feared the face he would see would be Fulgrim's, his father toying with him, come again to take his life. He felt vitality fleeing him, drawn through the fiery umbilical back into the thing as it revealed itself.

It was not Fulgrim.

Eidolon's own face stared back at him, unruined by time or circumstance, bearing all its old strength and beauty and arrogance. Fire still burned in its eyes, rings of captive light thrumming within the coils of its irises.

'It is so very good, my brother,' the other soul purred, *'to be with you once again.'*

SIXTEEN

WAR OF BROTHERS

The battle lines had fragmented. There was no front. There was not even truly an enemy any longer. No friends. No allies. Only war.

Vocipheron scrambled over the hull of a ruined tank and leapt down onto a pile of rubble, hunting through the murk. What had once been a mighty intersection, moving men and materiel from the outer defences to the city's heart, had collapsed in on itself. The dead were everywhere – crushed by debris, sprawled across makeshift medicae stations, or ground underfoot or undertread.

So much death. And yet none of it mattered.

Vocipheron's men were all but gone and so he hunted his prey with bestial abandon, uncaring of where they were. It was not the patient battle of the duellist any more. He had been reduced to the barest sense of awareness, an animal cognition that spoke to some ancient reptilian-hindbrain urge.

One of his blades was gone, lost somewhere in the unceasing madness of the war.

'Prey?' Alef snapped and snarled. The warrior's pristine features were wracked by palsy, split with new scars where he had etched or clawed at his skin. He sniffed the air and hissed like a canid.

'Soon,' Vocipheron growled back before the red-and-black blindness reared up in his skull once more. 'He is near. He must be.'

He had been a fool, he realised. The sudden epiphany had swept him as surely as the muscle spasms and moments of fugue. It was as obvious and as revelatory as the great column of warp fire that scraped the sky, clawing its way up from the core of the dead fortress, guided by the King's incomparable song. The wind rang with strange melodies from other times and places, weeping through into reality with a wistful longing. An urge at last satiated.

There had been some mechanism here, he saw that now. Something hidden behind the veil. A lock that the steady shedding of blood had loosened. Eidolon, somehow, had been the key.

Now there was only the hunt. Only the reckoning.

Vocipheron had watched, weeping behind his helm, as the first of the Dark Prince's handmaidens had appeared, bleeding from shadows and out of arches to nowhere. Hooved feet stamped at the ground as they began their dance, weaving through half-collapsed corridors and out into the debris-choked thoroughfares. His eyes followed their inconstant courses, catching upon flailing fabric and pierced flesh, their violet skin marked with mutilations and violations that put the Emperor's Children's best efforts to shame.

Unclean light bled from their wounds and alterations – an unbiological luminescence, a wrongness wrought from iridescence. It hurt to look at them. Everything was pain. His mania was a knife drawn along his spine, flensing away the flesh and etching the bone.

Much as, he realised, the daemons were doing to the mortal

remains that decorated the city's corpse. They set upon the bodies with claw and knife, tooth and needle. Bull-headed god-things strung flayed flesh between ornaments of chiselled bone, while others coaxed bloody trees to flex and grow from the gardens of ribcages and entrails. The daemonettes cooed and whispered, darting from growth to growth, claws snapping out to cleave newly formed flesh flowers from the boughs.

Somewhere a bell had begun to toll, its ringing trapped within his skull, making his vision swim with nausea. Bile sang in his throat, a momentary spike of acid before he hunched forwards once more and let the growl escape his lips.

Hunger joined the pain. Not for the tawdry constructs of the daemonic but for true flesh and blood. His eyes darted, chasing shadows as the fires raged above and beyond him. The warp's sick light stained everything, vying with the warring starships above.

The overhead lumens had died. All light, natural and artificial, had died only to be replaced by the *unnatural*.

He pushed himself up by the blade-tip, still hunched over, his shoulders shaking with sudden bursts of savage laughter. There were tears upon his cheeks as he wept spontaneously. He was losing control of everything; every part of him was in utter rebellion. All that mattered was the desire, the need to indulge himself. To kill and maim and feast upon what remained.

His hearing realigned and his head snapped up like that of a hunting dog, eager for the chase. Bolter fire and sonic weaponry discharged nearby, drawing his attention. The night came alive with roars and screams, the howls of battle and stunted mewling as his brothers indulged themselves amidst the wreckage of the city.

He had to find him, Vocipheron realised. Malakris. There were reckonings yet to be had. 'Where are you, brother?' he screamed. 'Come out and let us finish this!'

* * *

Malakris looked up from the Son of Horus who had, until quite
recently, been languishing under his attentions. His claws were
slick with transhuman blood, jammed through empty sockets
and out of the ruptured bone at the back of the warrior's skull.

He withdrew them with exaggerated slowness and looked
around.

The enemy lay, half slumped, over an ornamental fountain,
his entrails staining the water with blood and filth. Scum had
begun to gather around the sea-green armour, a distasteful froth
that wormed its way into every crack and wound. The scent of
it was utterly delectable. Had there been time he might have cut
a flank free and feasted upon the flesh, or perhaps restrained
himself to the offal like some hive-nobility gourmand.

There would be opportunities enough later. When the enemy
were dead and all were merely chattel at his feet. When the
whispers had delivered their promises, then there would be
time for all his desires to be sated.

Few obstacles remained. The world was screaming, raging
and burning with the warp's fury, the whispers turned shrill
and high. Eidolon caged in fire, both Legions scattered upon
the wind.

Rise and stand as a prince of war. Master of the Third Millen-
nial. All the old shall be swept away! Kill him and none shall
blunt your ascension.

Somewhere Rykan Bail was screaming. The warrior howled
and cackled as he vaulted over a piece of ruined statuary, perch-
ing like a gargoyle atop half of an ornamental bench, clawing
at it with his power fist. The madness was no longer subtle. He
wore it plainly for all to see. A sign and a symbol for the others
of their warband to follow.

Soon there would be a true challenge, Malakris knew.

Every ruler had his inheritors and Eidolon was no different.
He had carved out his place by will alone. Why should Malakris

not follow in the lord commander's footsteps? It would not be the broken monster that was Plegua, nor the stubborn fool Vocipheron. Even the equerry could be dealt with. One at a time. Blow by blow and claw by claw.

The curved talons flexed with need, quivering at the thought.

There was a beauty and a power in betrayal. They had learned that at Isstvan, both times they had been called to the Warmaster's battles. Whether slaying brothers or cousins, the undertaking was still sweet. Dread Slaanesh, youngest and yet eternal, had shown them the joys and delights that lay in treachery.

To give in and never die.

Muscles bunched and seized beneath his skin as a fresh palsy swept through him. Malakris rolled his shoulders and turned from the Son of Horus, who still lay dead, blinded, uncaring of the wider war that he had failed to win.

Malakris would carve his way through those who opposed him until he was so suffused with glory that even the Phoenician would take notice of him.

'There will be one more king amidst the ashes,' he muttered to himself. He tried to signal his men again, but there was no response. The damned interference was still occluding the vox. He strode over and seized the sides of Bail's head, forcing the madman to look at him.

'And this time,' he went on, 'I will rise and never fall.'

SEVENTEEN

SOULBOUND

It wore his past like a mockery, cloaked in all that he had been.

The Eidolon that looked back, flickers of flame still crawling across its skin and armour, was beautiful. Perfect. It was everything that he had been before Fulgrim's wrath had sundered him. There was no ugly scar across the throat, no wan skin or lank hair. It stalked and preened about the figmented space with a pure arrogance and an ephemeral beauty.

Eidolon remembered that power and surety. He had thought it long lost to him, and while he was no longer the shambling horror that Fulgrim had disdained as *stupid and ugly*, he was still a shadow of his former self. His powers were ascendant, true enough. He had thought himself capable of running down the Khan at Kalium. He would have triumphed, he knew that in his shattered soul. He would have broken the Warhawk and eaten his heart, carved a throne from his iron-hard bones.

Yet I could be more. We could be more. If I had not passed beyond death, then what? Would an unbroken Eidolon have risen to yet greater heights? Would I stand alongside Julius, the Favoured Son, if I had not earned the ire of Fulgrim's whim?

What would I be? Who would I have become?

'What are you?'

'*I am your brother,*' it laughed. '*And I am you. When Fulgrim took you from your life, when he unmade you, the very power of the anathame shattered our soul.*'

'Our soul?' Eidolon asked.

'*Our soul,*' it repeated. '*Your title is not an idle boast, Soul-Severed.*' Something hateful moved behind its eyes, a dark mockery and a burning, perpetual envy. '*We are two sides of the same coin, you and I. Cut from the same cloth and yoked to different destinies. One bound to the flesh–*'

'And the other to the warp,' he concluded.

The perfect vision of his soul shimmered, its radiance refracted as though through a thousand broken mirrors. Light of every hue shone through its skin and armour till it seemed ablaze again. Gold burned with internal fire, running and flowing into new shapes and configurations, warped and spread like constellations across the rich purple plate.

'*The sea of souls is a cruel mistress, but there are lessons in the flame.*' It held out one flawless gauntlet, inspecting the fingers one by one. It looked at Eidolon again and its jaws widened into a vast grin, teeming with extra teeth. Each was sharp and blindingly white. '*And yet I see that the physical realm has also been unkind.*'

'I have survived,' Eidolon said as he circled the other figure, gripping his hammer tightly. 'Thrived, even. I enjoy more power and ability than before my...' He faltered. 'Before my humbling. Now there is strength and vigour in me as I have never known. I feel...' Eidolon paused, reaching out to claw at the empty air as though grasping for an idea.

'*As though you could challenge the child-gods themselves,*' it burbled, amusedly. *'Perhaps you could. Maybe the Phoenician would find himself dying beneath your blows, rather than the reverse. Or would you rather the Khan be humbled? The Praetorian shattered? The Great Angel's wings trodden beneath your conquering boots? Such delights. Wonders and splendours in equal measure. To crack a primarch's bones and drain their marrow. We could do these things. **Together.***'

'You think I need you?' Eidolon said, yet his voice was uncertain. He remembered what it was to be whole, defined by his skill and ability, not by the eternal pain.

'I do not think you need anything, brother. I think you desire much and more. You could stand as a Legion Master in your own right. We both remember how the Legion was, in its infancy. Small and yet so determined. It was not Fulgrim who saved us. Fabius remade the Legion just as he remade us. It was the will of our warriors and the wishes of the gods that saved us from oblivion.'

'Saying it does not make it so,' Eidolon snarled. He strode forward, face to face with himself.

As he spoke, the stone behind him changed and became the shimmering crystal coral that had once formed the atolls of Laeran. His doppelganger reached out and stroked the coral, and it writhed beneath the Shattered King's touch. It began to thrum gently, ringing with a song that was beautifully familiar and yet horrifically alien.

The song. The Eternal Song. The song of the Dark Prince. No… the call of the Shattered King. The glory they would wield together.

'Yes,' the soul burred. *'You remember its power and its wonder.'*

'I remember,' Eidolon breathed.

'That power could be ours again. It should be ours.' It reached out and took hold of Eidolon's hand. The Lord Commander Primus could feel the dull ache as fire climbed his limb, drowning it in gnawing pain. *'Power is the inheritance of those worthy*

enough to claim it. With our soul reunited, we would create such black miracles as the galaxy has never seen. We could transcend the petty limitations placed upon us and rise without limit. A phoenix in truth.'

Eidolon's grip faltered and he stumbled back. He looked down at the twisted fingers of his gauntlet, at the beautiful legacy of Horvia, and blinked momentarily. The digits had blackened and faded, like an overexposed pict. Vitality seeped away from him, just as surely as the pink hue of his armour.

'You could be so beautiful,' it sighed. *'Let me show you.'*

It raised its hand and drew the fingers down the side of Eidolon's face, the gentle sensation suddenly erupting into a migraine-flare of absolute agony. His eyes snapped shut and yet he still saw. Saw:

The fire within becoming a raging inferno, burning through his veins and arteries, climbing his nerves in a cascade of scintillating black flames. Bones cracking and reshaping beneath the furnace heat as he became more than merely a man, a sun trapped in a cage of bone, an inferno in human skin. A burnt offering before the altars of the gods.

Eidolon died and was born again. Caught in an eternal cycle he could never escape, remade and reshaped by strength of soul alone. His armour broke apart and reknit as though returned to the armouring serfs and thralls.

He was the anvil now. He was the hammer. Trying to scream through a throat that would not, could not, make human sounds. Unspeech poured from him, gouting from his lips like blood, stretching out as it became coherent and material in the dizzying unreality of the warp. He could break reality with words alone. He was an unmaker king, burning with the light that had been kindled long before humanity was even dreamt of.

It tore him apart at the molecular level before it forced him back together in strange configurations. His spirit caught between apotheosis and utter dissolution.

For a second, reality threatened to fragment, to force him to watch his gifts spill out in a rush of horror and warp-maddened flesh, but it held. The light within was all-consuming now, searing through him. His armour shone.

This was the power the Phoenician would deny them, hiding in his palaces of delusion.

Golden claws flexed open and closed. His hammer had changed, exalted into an immense gold-headed maul, crawling with blazing symbols. His fangs gnashed together and a tongue, forked and barbed, slid from between them. His skin was rich violet, perfect and unmarked. He had become as close to a god as he would ever be, removed from the realm of the flesh, elevated to a Great Game he had only begun to understand the rules of.

Reality asserted itself once more in a cold wave of pressure. Next to the exquisite rapture of the vision of ascension, it was a hollow sensation. Pleasure bled away from him, a slow deadening of the nerves spreading out from the blackened hand. He tasted a universe without joy or carnage.

The beautiful war they had been promised, an end to the Emperor's restrictive tyranny and all the petty banalities... It would slip from his fingers.

'If we were whole, we could rise...'

'Yes, rise! We would be as we were always intended to be. A warrior.'

'A warrior of the gods,' Eidolon whispered thoughtfully. The vision clung to him, poisoning every thought with its power and fury. He could feel the galaxy quaking beneath his feet, as though in waiting.

'Horus Lupercal's war has made us all the swords of the gods. Their gifts fuel us to new heights. That is the power that shall break the Emperor's walls and shatter the Palace. Only in the warp are such things made holy.'

'Our new gods have given us much.' Eidolon hesitated. Flashes returned to him in the interstitial space between life and death, between materium and immaterium.

Claws tearing him apart as surely as the anathame's keen edge. Laughter ringing about him like the mirth of the gods themselves. Split apart, thought and memory torn asunder.

'They have also taken,' he concluded.

'Then let us undo their work. There does not have to be discord between us, my brother. Merely let me back in. Open your flesh to my glory and together we shall be unstoppable.'

'Open my flesh to you?' Eidolon paused.

'One body and one soul. Your physicality bound again to my transcendent power. Then we shall be complete.'

Surrender... the voice breathed, rising in a chorus of whispers to surround him. He could hear the word, repeated over and over, driven into his mind like a needle.

They would be strong together. Powerful enough to seize the Legion itself. To rise above his flawed flesh, and to truly ascend. To thrive. To attain the primacy he had always deserved.

They have also taken.

Eidolon swallowed hard.

'You would have me *surrender* to you?' Eidolon growled suddenly. The coral of Laeran cracked and fell away. The rearing barbs of Murder's corpse-trees rose about them now, closing in, hooking at their flesh. The perfect and the imperfect were caught upon them, blood staining the pale skin.

Torgaddon's taunts rang in his ears. The petulant defiance of Tarvitz. The arrogant smirk of Lucius.

The weakness of others. That is forever the failing.

He looked at the perfect rendition of his soul. Madness and yearning danced in its eyes. More than that, a hungry desperation. The absolute need. The *arrogance*. He remembered it well. How it had felt to be so sure in his own power, and to know nothing but the craving for more.

Had he been more then, or less?

For Eidolon, death had not been an end but a beginning. An opportunity seized with bloody hands. He had faltered for a time and sought a cure, an answer. A fool's hope. Not because it could not be done but because he had realised it was not necessary.

I have never known myself more than when I was broken. Made glorious in ruin, just as our Legion has been.

Eidolon drove his fist into its breastplate, forcing it back further into the branches, anointing him in agony. 'Perhaps I should simply take your power instead?' His throat trilled, pulsing as though about to unleash his scream. Eidolon bit back his rage and forced a smile. 'If I seize your strength, what do we become then? Do you think I will allow myself to be ruled by a weaker aspect of myself? You fled from us, severed or not. You gave in. Surrendered to the warp. You were weak.'

'Be silent!' it hissed. For a moment the perfect facade cracked, and the true horror bled through. Its skin was deathly pale and stretched taut over its skull, black lips drawn back from sharp teeth. It wore a parody of Astartes plate, clicking and worn, broken by geologic ages spent in torment. Claw gouges marked it, over and over, like a primitive's attempt at keeping time. The purple had been chiselled away and the gilding was merely a memory.

Eidolon did not recoil. He pushed himself away from it, moving back with practised ease. Creating distance between himself and the thing that called him brother.

He stared at the warped remnant of his soul, seeing it at last as it truly was. Horror, even by the standards of the III Legion. Not because it was monstrous but because it was a surrender to monstrosity.

'You did not have to be as you have become,' Eidolon sneered. 'Better you had surrendered to dissolution than allowed yourself to become nothing more than their plaything.'

'I am not a puppet!' his soul snarled. Its immaterial form shuddered and twisted, moving in a heat blur, a sodium light smear across the liminal space. It threw itself forward and clawed for him. Talons of black fire tore at his armour, and Eidolon hissed in pain where they found purchase.

And then it was gone.

Sensation bled away, stolen by the creature's longing. Eidolon's armour blackened and cracked. He could feel the skin below doing the same. A flash of agony, and then nothing. Nerves withered beneath the onslaught, taking the gift the Dark Prince had conveyed to him. The Eternal Song of creation stuttered and died away, replaced by the horrific yawning silence of the tomb. The grand symphony fled him.

Shadows and fire swirled about him, a closing vortex driving itself between the tombstones of memory. Eidolon spun and swung his hammer through the gloom, its flickering head failing to dispel the darkness.

The King hurled itself from the black.

The daemonic echo of his soul grinned, its teeth a nest of rot and ruin. Vitality surged up its outstretched arm, renewing and remaking it. The flickering image stabilised, and the perfect illusion returned.

'I never wanted it to be this way, brother. I wanted you to yield to me. You could have known the pleasures that Slaanesh prepared for you. Agony and ecstasy such as you have never known.'

Eidolon drew his arm back sharply and raised the hammer once more. 'You will not have my flesh. If you want it, then you will have to tear it from me.'

Black fire kindled at the daemon-form's fingertips, flowing into a new configuration. Shadows danced about it, becoming solid. The blackened spur of tormented reality shattered and realigned.

Eidolon let a bitter laugh slip from his lips as he watched the spectral weapon coalesce. The shadows and flame assumed a familiar form. He could picture it in motion...

Sweeping for his throat in a glittering arc of dead stone and cutting edge. The relic-weapon of revelation. A sword that had shed the blood of the Warmaster himself.

Eidolon's body shuddered spontaneously, wracked by death-spasm memories. The echo of the anathame came up as the enemy tipped it in a mocking salute.

'You remember this, yes?' it cooed as it moved forwards. The pale features twisted into a mask of pain and hate. *'The pain of it has haunted you, but it became a part of me. I suffered and broke, while Fabius dragged you back to life. You had your second chance. Dancing to Fulgrim's tune. Midwifing his ascension, with no thought to your own!'*

'I have earned my place amongst the Legion. No matter the jackals that snap at my heels. I brought a third of them to my number. I lead as we march upon Terra. Let the others prattle and feud. I am beyond them. If there is any merit to the quest for perfection, then I have embraced and exceeded it.'

The last word poured from him in a psychosonic scream. The daemon-soul winced and stumbled backwards. The blade clenched in its grip lost coherency with a weak scream of its own. Eidolon took *Glory Aeterna* in both hands and readied it. 'Come, weakling. I will test my skill against myself. Let us see if our flesh or spirit is the stronger!'

Almost as one, the two opposing halves hurled themselves forward in a flare of light and shadow.

EIGHTEEN

MONSTERS AND KIN

Plegua stumbled and weaved through the madness, chasing the centre of the song.

Perhaps in time he would truly ascend to the Dark Prince's mysteries, and this would be as mere instinct. He could feel the changes in the song. The subtle aches and shifts. Flashes of things that were not quite visions, sieved through the lord commander's pain.

The sting of clawed fingers as they traced the scrimshawed revels upon his half-face, displayed like a carnival masque for the final feast to come.

He shook himself from dreams and hefted his weapon-instrument once more. He sighted and fired, and created art.

Opha Demaskos vaulted over a pile of steaming rubble and died screaming in mid-air. The sonic blast caught him and held him for one beautiful moment, as every molecule in his being vibrated. Coherence persisted, struggled to maintain itself, and then came apart. Blood fountained from every seam of his armour. The plates burst apart and shattered. The seals at each joint atomised. He was still howling as he died, his lunatic euphoria subsumed into the song.

'Forwards,' Plegua rumbled.

Von Kalda nodded and followed, firing as he went. His other hand was occupied with the narthecium mechanisms bolted into his wrist. Occasionally he would pause and introduce a new chemical element into Plegua's straining system, mediating the war between stimulants and pain-goads.

Plegua had found him in the roiling insanity, hunched over in some ornamental garden, chest heaving with the strain of resisting. Von Kalda had already saturated his own system with calmatives, struggling to hold his ravaged psyche together. Plegua could taste the chemicals on the air, bleeding from Von Kalda's pores, warring with the adrenaline surging through the equerry's tortured physique.

'Forwards,' he whispered in agreement. Each word was a struggle, forced through gritted teeth.

'The heart of the fortress bleeds. Collapsing. Down into the pit he goes. Down with the King amidst the ashes.' Plegua's voice was almost a sing-song as he parsed the furious power of the warp, drawing his verse from the universe's sick skin.

Von Kalda nodded his assent as Plegua led him on, pausing now and then to guide him by the shoulder, as he might the blind or the lost. The last traces of the Lord Commander Primus' presence lay towards the core, where Eidolon had advanced up the centre to meet Gherog, spear-tip to spear-tip.

Always such an arrogant creature, Plegua mused, *and yet he has the right. He is our lord. The firstborn of the Kakophoni. Fabius' triumph.* There was enough left of Plegua that remembered what it meant to be a soldier rather than a weapon. So many of them had given in, surrendered to become nothing more than instruments in the Eternal Song.

Just as his brothers had surrendered. Given in to the terrible melody that now howled from the fortress ruins.

The Neverborn were everywhere now. Conducting their own choirs and performances from the ruins of battlements and habs. Human corpses, claw-ravaged and broken, hung from the windows, impaled upon glass, strung from gibbets for the amusements of the Dark Gods. Vast, swollen monsters, their horned heads bound with leather straps, held court in burning armouries and presided over meat foundries into which lifeless bodies were poured.

He wished he had time. He could kneel at the feet of such beings. He could learn new pleasures and sing new songs of boundless suffering. He could. He should–

No.

'Keep moving,' he growled. 'This is not how our song ends.'

The descent was pain.

The pit was not a natural formation. It had no natural origin. To his eyes it seemed acid-etched into the world, wracked by vulgar flame and edged in obsidian. Balefire licked at the heavens in green infernos. Violet plumes danced amidst the strangely angled cave formations. At the core of the great shaft a vast spear of warp light scraped at the heavens, blazing like a beacon, resonating like the symphony at the end of all things.

Vocipheron snarled and yanked his eyes away, panting like a hound, acid saliva pouring from his lips.

The Legion was dying around them. He had not seen a living Son of Horus in… How long had it been? How long had they been fighting? How long had he been hunting?

It did not matter. Only the prey mattered.

He is weak. He is killing the Third Millennial. I will make him see.

Malakris was somewhere below, capering from ledge to ledge, all decency forgotten. He had to be punished. Made to repent his petty vanities. Something at the back of his skull hissed and whispered, insistent that one or both should die. Offered up as a sacrifice. Nothing more than sensation for the rites.

His sword scraped the rock, seeking purchase as he readied himself. He vaulted to a lower echelon. Vocipheron could hear the laughter from below. It would not be long now.

Soon he would have what he desired most. The pain and pleasure would abate and there would only be the glory of the moment.

'Now, my brothers!' he called, and somewhere behind him Alef and the others snarled their own responses. 'We end him here and now!'

The pit embraced him as a lover, welcomed him with all the pain and pleasure he expected.

The world beneath the world was a sacred thing now, shaped by the will of the gods alone. Fire clawed its way skyward, lighting him in its mad hues. The colours of his armour had run and shifted; the daemon blood he had daubed himself in responded to its source, coming alive once more. It crooned to him, assuring him his choice was correct.

He could feel the pulse and thrum of it, the warp's mad song finally given voice.

Everything rang with the Shattered King's laughter, with the screams and howls that he could swear belonged to the Lord Commander Primus. This had been his doing, Malakris realised. On some level, Eidolon's very presence had brought this into being.

They were bound together, Eidolon and the dying world. He had risen to power here. Perhaps that power had scarred them both… A wound in soul and reality that the warp could exploit.

Down into the pit's depths he descended. Others followed him. He could not be sure of their numbers or allegiance. Circling down towards the glories that awaited. He could smell the potential that dwelt below, so close, and yet so far!

Malakris hit the ground running, finally at the base of the great gouge in the earth. The others followed him. Bail was right behind him, alongside five others. A meagre pack, but enough for their purposes.

The warp's caustic touch had eaten away at the roots of the Palace Militant like acid, cutting and working with the skill of the infinite. The pit felt like a suppurating lesion, cut into the world by the inelegant scalpel of the immaterium. It put him in mind of a meteor crater, biting deep into the planet's crust.

He beheld the fruit of that labour now.

The rift itself was a sphere of unreality, a pulsing sore that seemed at once void and yet possessed a disturbing solidity. It nestled where it had fallen, drawing errant debris into its hungry maw. Malakris drew nearer, claws raised. To touch it, to pass through, to cut his way in. He could hear the screaming agony of its very existence. His teeth hurt just to stand near to it.

Another howl cut through the tumult and he spun about, claws raised and crossed.

Malakris turned aside the sweep of Vocipheron's blade, joy-mad and shrilling as he did.

'Brother!' he cackled.

The swordsman did not answer. All of the warrior's restraint had been ripped away. He carried only the one sword, swinging it like a berserker. Malakris capered back, driving his claws into the other warrior's side. More of Vocipheron's ragged host descended, hurling themselves at the hedonists with wild abandon. Brothers brawled, tearing at each other. Swords split faces and cut across stomachs in disembowelling strokes. Claws and mauls cracked plate.

Malakris watched Rykan Bail seize one of Vocipheron's lieutenants by the helm and squeeze, crushing it in a shower of blood and bone with his power fist.

'Is this not wonderful?' Malakris taunted. 'This is the feast we were always meant for, my brother! This is what victory tastes like! This is all I ever wanted for you. For you to see the beauty of it!'

Vocipheron's eyes were wild, his features locked in a hateful rictus. It broke for a single second. The sword came round again, nicking Malakris at the throat. He tasted blood, felt it run down the inside of his armour.

'There he is!' Malakris screamed. 'Show me your true colours, swordsman. Show me what all that aesthete's restraint hides!'

The great beacon rift blazed behind them, shuddering with every blow. Reality moved and swayed with their colliding weapons. Brothers locked in mortal conflict tumbled apart in another pulse of light. The shadows dissipated and Neverborn concubines slid from the darkness, claws clacking as they applauded the riotous bloodshed and suffering that now abounded.

Something yearned to be born, feeding on their sorrows and their pain.

Don't feed it. Stop this… something pleaded in the recesses of his mind.

One of the daemonettes looked skyward. Eyes narrowing, lip curling as her claws came up in a futile gesture of warding.

The figure that descended was immense, its bulk slamming through her in a burst of perfumed ichor. It did not falter or hesitate. It swung its weapon around in a great circular arc. Astartes warriors hit the walls as a wave of sound drove them back. Malakris went to one knee. He could taste blood again. His lip had split. He felt the warm liquid flowing from his eyes, nose and ears.

Vocipheron staggered back, standing only because he had dug his sword into the earth, clinging to it like a drowning man to driftwood.

NINETEEN

SOUL AND MEMORY

Light and shadow met, filling the confines of the warp space
with fitful lightning.

The weapon was not the true anathame. It possessed none of
its coiled malice, the sentience that waited, coaxed into a neme-
sis edge. This was an echo. A shadow. An appropriate weapon
for the thing that aped Eidolon's might and glory.

Yet it was fast. Potent with desperation. Determined to fight
and die rather than be reduced to a waiting phantom, desperate to reclaim the flesh. If Eidolon refused it, defeated it,
what would become of it then? Would it linger and then seize
some other brother's body?

Each collision of weapons sent yet more maddened light
flowing around its edges, catching on the facets of the space
as though it were some great jewel.

'I am all you could have been!' it hissed.

Eidolon drove it back, swinging his hammer in great killing

arcs. It hit some imagined wall, and a new reality blossomed around them.

The virus-spawned ashes of Isstvan III pooled around their ankles, clinging to them with a cloying need. Eidolon spat to one side and ducked away from another sword-stroke. He looked around at the tableau of his living memory. Some was as he remembered. The frustration and stymied assaults. Lucius and his arrogant presumption. Victory thanks to the machinations of another, motivated by nothing more than arrogance and pride. All for a chance to sit in glory. Honour and integrity had lost their lustre by then, but the hypocrisy of it yet rankled.

He blinked and the image changed. He saw himself leading the *defence*. Defiant before his fellows. Loyal, as though the title meant anything.

'*Roads not taken*,' it burbled. '*The warp's gift.*' It swung for him with the shadow anathame, and the weapons met again in a screech of black lightning.

The world convulsed. The ashes were suddenly the pall of black sand. Isstvan V blossomed about them. He laughed and then let his throat sacs swell. His scream cut across the new wonder and horror. He could hear it again. The song echoed about them. Voiced from thousands of throats, carried in every last bolt-round as they detonated, every sword-stroke and death.

He channelled it and bound it in his scream, driving it through the daemonic form. It howled as it came apart, carried on the ash wind, circling him like a cyclone as the images faded and shifted.

Upon every facet of the warp prison, his life played out. As it was. As it could be. He saw himself distended and swollen by the empyrean, rising on pinions of fire, howling his own apotheosis. Eidolon saw himself at the head of the Legion entire, crowned with Fulgrim's mark and the sigil of the Dark Prince. The sweep of his hammer was a trail of black fire. The walls of the Palace were aflame under his advance. He saw himself casting Dorn from the walls, triumphant as he did so, euphoric as he rose.

The whisper of flame was at his back, and he spun. It reformed, a cackling shadow made of fire and hate. The shadow blade plunged.

Eidolon roared in fury as it impaled him through his upper chest, pinning him to one of the false realities. Cracks spiderwebbed across the images, shattering them further, breaking apart each potential history into yet more varied configurations. The daemon-soul grinned wolfishly and pushed harder. Crimson welled around the blade's edges, pouring through the rent in the armour, soaking his flesh with spilled lifeblood. Light flowed after it, draining away into the depths of the sword.

Eidolon pushed himself up, tried to bring the hammer to bear, but its hand shot out and seized Eidolon's. Bones cracked in its grip, and he let go of the hammer.

'*This*,' it whispered as it lifted the hammer reverently, watching *Glory Aeterna* shimmer with the fire of Eidolon's dying soul. '*This belongs to me. Everything you are, Lord Commander Primus, belongs to me.*' It looked at Eidolon one last time, as though he were filth upon its boot, and then kicked the dying lord commander back into the flickering dust.

They were bound, in the dying dreamscape, caught by competing umbilicals of soul-light and shadow. Seconds passed, metastasising into minutes, as the daemon-form swelled and revitalised. New fire kindled across the plates of its armour. It cascaded into new configurations, twisting and writhing, hands locked upon the hammer's haft. In one instant it was a perfect creature, its armour the flawless work of master artificers, the weapon it held still beautiful. The next, it had become truly daemonic, the first steps along a road that would only end with them subsumed by the warp. Burning with the black flame at creation's end. Alive and undying in a way Eidolon could never be alone.

He could feel his life ebbing away. The shadow blade had bitten deep, and Eidolon thought of Perturabo, his vitality stolen to fuel Fulgrim's ascent. His mind quested, touching the dreamscape. Glittering fragments began to rain around them. Eidolon blinked, forcing his breath through his teeth.

The bounty of Prismatica drifted around them in eddies and drifts of brilliant iridescence, just as they had at the offering upon Iydris. He sighed. Brilliant shards filled the skies. Eidolon let his mind soar, his memories coming alive.

The frozen forests of Europa rose around him now. His rival, his opposite, was too distracted, glorying in the stolen life force, drawing Eidolon's power to it. Through it. Eidolon forced his hand up haltingly and took hold of the anathame's hilt.

Who are you? a voice burred from the infinite void around them, echoing between the petrified trunks. *When it matters, who are you? Will you lie down and die? Surrender? Merely the spare son of a dying lineage? Or will you fight? Triumph? Rule?*

He felt the memory become real once more. Fingers closing about his chin, tilting his vision up. He almost laughed.

*Become who you were always meant to be, **my son**.*

He knew the voice. Intimately. He expected, as his gaze tilted, to see the pale features of his father.

There was only darkness. Only pain. Eidolon knew that pain well, its presence as familiar as Fulgrim's hissing voice. He felt his fingers lock tight around the false anathame's hilt.

Eidolon pulled the blade free and smiled his bloody smile.

It turned a second too late. Eidolon threw himself forward, shoulder-charging the monstrous simulacrum into a waiting pillar, driving it through it. Stone shards and dust tumbled from its form, dousing the flames, turning the armour ash grey. It hissed, and the daemon bled through once more. Eidolon drove his boot down and pinned the hammer across its chest, trapping it.

'You have not earned this!' he snarled. He dropped low and seized the hammer, pulling it back even as he drove the false sword down and through the Neverborn's chest. Pinning it to the ground. New strength flooded through him, sanctifying him in the moment. He could take all of its power. He could be whole again.

Eidolon paused. That was what all of this had been leading to. Whatever forces were manipulating them, whatever gods or demigods moved in the heavens, had arranged this... This was the end they desired.

He looked down at the fragment of his soul. Warp-sick and demented, screaming and howling its vengeance. Bloodshot eyes flickered and darted, seeking some final gambit. A last way out.

Eidolon lifted his hammer.

'I dedicate this death,' he whispered, 'to Slaanesh. I give of myself to the Dark Prince. I would sacrifice anything for the right to lead. I give myself, soul-severed and broken, to you, as long as the gods demand.'

The hammer fell. The daemon screamed. Everything quivered and came apart, shattering into so many spinning, glittering shards. The pasts and futures, the could-have-been and the never-were, died around them.

Eidolon closed his eyes and began to scream, as the fire flared bright and consumed them all.

TWENTY

LESSONS FROM THE ASHES

The warp's touch and the dying rift had wormed their way down into the flesh of the world, rendering the walls smooth and flowing like flash-frozen water. Eidolon blinked away the after-images of places that no longer existed, a tapestry wrought from memory and now swept aside by martial prowess and the whim of a god. He breathed in the stink of the pit and the indelible taste of reality once more.

He braced a hand against his armour. He was flesh again. Clad in his plate. Carrying his weapon. He did not feel an absence in his soul, merely… strength. Power. When he moved, it was in perfect concert with his will. Eidolon laughed quietly to himself and cast his eye about him, seeking the source of an echoing applause.

Malakris and Vocipheron had fallen to their knees amidst the calumny. One of Malakris' clawed gauntlets was braced against Vocipheron's wounded shoulder plate. Their chests heaved with exaggerated effort as the armour translated their exhaustion. Plegua stood over them, weapon still readied. Poised for whatever convulsion of violence greeted them next. Von Kalda knelt nearby, tending to a brother's wounds. The Astartes was pale, face streaked with blood from his eyes and nose. Silent. Weakened. Perhaps even dying.

Eidolon forced himself forwards, staggering as his strength ebbed. He pulled Malakris up, dislodging him from his fellow legionary.

'You are a weak-willed fool,' Eidolon said at last. Malakris spat to one side, his acid saliva streaked with blood.

'You wound me, lord.'

Eidolon's backhand caught him by surprise, bowling him over into the ashes. He rolled, sprawling over a mutilated corpse in purple and white. Its face had been gnawed off, though whether by the Neverborn or its fellow warriors of the III, Eidolon could not tell. Malakris forced himself back up and ignited his claws, standing and panting before the Lord Commander Primus as others gathered around him.

Eidolon ducked low and pinned Malakris to the ground by the throat. He braced himself about the captain's legs, forcing him down into the blood and ruin of their dead. *Glory Aeterna* was in his hand again, already ignited. Lightning danced between the active field and the madman's flesh, sizzling with a satisfying hiss of cooking meat.

'Once, you embraced this pain,' Eidolon snarled. He pushed harder. One of the barbed studs set in Malakris' face ceased quivering and began to run, leaving a trail of molten metal burning down his cheek. The captain's nerves finally overloaded and he began at last to scream.

The weapon started to obliterate his face. Moment by moment. Micron by micron. A wet *pop* resounded as one of Malakris' eyes burst, weeping blood and humour. He mewled and writhed piteously, his armoured bulk slamming against the ground of the great command hall.

'My lord.'

Eidolon snapped around and glared at the speaker. His rage faded for a moment, replaced by surprise as he realised who had addressed him. Vocipheron was still on his knees, his hair matted to his head with sweat, as though the climb had been a true test of his strength. His sword lay before him, the flawless sabre beautiful amidst the horror of the chamber. Like a memory of an idealised age.

'Spare him, lord.'

'Spare him?' Eidolon surged up, swinging the hammer about one-handed, pointing it at Vocipheron accusingly. 'Your petty rival? A man who could not hold himself together long enough for a simple prosecution?' He leant down, coming face to face with Vocipheron. The swordsman's flawless demeanour had cracked and whatever madness he had been struggling to keep sequestered had poured out. His hair was ragged and blood-smeared where he had torn at it. Long gouges marked his cheeks where he had clawed at his skin. Trophies had been pinned or nailed to his armour, cut free from the living and the dead alike.

'We will need every blade at Terra, Lord Commander Primus,' Vocipheron said, and shook his head. 'I despise him, but none of us were immune to the powers unleashed here. No matter what we pretend to be, we have all failed. If the Phoenician wished him dead, he would have struck him down himself.' The swordsman paused. 'If he is to die then let him die upon Terra's soil. Let him lay down his life before the walls of the Palace. There, at least, he will be of some use.'

'Mercy,' Malakris mewled from the ground. He had flipped over and forced himself onto all fours, hunched forward like an ailing canid. Drool and vomit dribbled from between his lips as he heaved and retched in agony. Eidolon's torment had robbed him of the joy that pain brought. Palsy swept him as he tried to rise unsteadily to his feet. He skidded and slipped on the entrail-slicked ground, bracing himself with his outstretched arms. 'I have served, lord, and I can be of service again. I ask only for the chance.'

Eidolon looked down at him for a long moment.

He turned and scanned the crowd. So few of the Third Millennial were gathered, cleaving to their makeshift warbands and shifting allegiances. Tathen Ord of the Ravager cadre, his shaven scalp carved with flowing symbols from a dead language. Caradar Fenek with his oiled locks and fierce eyes, lips constantly moving in a relentless recitation of poetry.

Then he saw Til Plegua, no longer lost to the rapture of the song. His eyes were fixed on Eidolon's, holding his gaze with his half-visage. The scrimshawed skull of half his face grinned in hollow longing at him, like a memento mori come to life. Beside him, almost in contrast, was the eternally youthful face of Von Kalda, his smooth cheeks reddened by the struggle.

Eidolon hesitated. He stepped forwards, hammer still raised, and looked down at Malakris. In judgement. How many lords and masters had he observed in the same situation? A noble standing sentinel over his lesser, nestled amidst the frozen forests of Europa, content to trade a child for security or for favour.

A primarch, doling out his affections and attentions with an even hand, even as he grew miserly with his trust. Fixated on a star he could never attain.

A lord commander, the fate of thousands trickling through his fingers, vying for power and position amongst rivals. Caught in the perpetual struggle of court politics and advancement.

What would I be without that struggle, the crucible that shaped me into this? One absent father or the one who made me as I am, time and again? In victory and defeat. Through life and death.

He closed his eyes. Mocking laughter echoed in the darkness. The twisted mirror of his own poisoned mirth, burbled through the lips of the Shattered King.

The judgement of our betters. The poison of mercy...

Eidolon opened his eyes. He reached out his free hand.

Malakris looked up at him, surprise writ across his face.

'Rise,' Eidolon said.

Someone began to applaud. He was not sure who. Eidolon turned and surveyed the tight confines of the pit. Now that the rift had burned itself out, the other warriors had spread out around the edges of it. Eidolon stood at its centre, turning his gaze from one warrior to the next, seeking whoever was clapping. Eager to cease the mockery.

None of them were moving.

Eidolon turned.

The sound rang strangely in the warp-worn space. Nightmares and echoes clung to every surface, resounding where they should die, taking form like dancing witch-fire. Light and shadow scrabbled along the obsidian-bladed edges of the pit, flickering and pulsing as though stirred by some great wind. He followed the sound to its source, and his breath caught in his throat.

The armoured figure was tall and lithe. The war plate that clung to him had been forged with superlative skill, work that spoke of the long toil of master craftsmen. The apex of humanity's artificers. White hair cascaded down his shoulders like an avalanche of purest snowfall. His skin was alabaster, and yet it shone from within like a captive star. His eyes were cruel and beautiful and sparkled with a seductive madness. Worlds had fallen into those eyes and torn themselves apart for but the smallest fragment of his regard.

He was art itself. A painting or a sculpture wrought by a savant and given life, like the Galateans of ancient myth. Yet he burned with vitality. Biology and spirituality had intersected perfectly for him to spring, fully formed, from some mortal godhead.

Fulgrim, the Phoenician himself, looked down upon Eidolon and ceased his applause.

'*My son,*' he breathed, the merest effort utterly melodic. There was venom layered there with the saccharine tones. Eidolon forced himself up, teeth gritted. There was pain, yes, but pain was his dear companion now. It sang in his blood and pirouetted in his soul. Without his pain he had thought that he was nothing. Now he had passed through the fire, and he knew better. He knew his own truth.

'Father,' Eidolon said. He could barely look at Fulgrim. Afterimages stalked the primarch as he moved, heat haze dogging his every step. Sometimes he was the great Illuminator as he had always been, and yet at other times…

The serpent of the apocalypse, body dragging itself forwards with inexorable longing, slouching towards inevitability, ever hungry and insatiable. Too many arms moving in impossible rhythm, each one carrying a blade from another dead culture.

He blinked away the daemonic vision and regarded his father as he had been in true life.

'*You surprise me, Eidolon. I did not expect you to take so readily to the game.*'

'The game?' Eidolon almost laughed. He strode towards his father and showed no fear. The immaterial afterbirth faded from around the Lord Commander Primus, and he stood to his full height. His fingers closed and opened, and he felt the new strength there. Power born of sacrifice.

'*It is all a game, my son. All of it. It ever has been. Since before this war began, we have been pieces upon the board.*' Fulgrim drew a long, straight blade from a human-leather scabbard and examined the edge of it, thoughtfully and longingly. '*Some of us have become players, in our time, of course. I was not content to watch from the sidelines while the war burned on and on… I have to test my sons to the best of their ability. Perhaps Julius will be next…*'

'You did this?' Eidolon said, aghast.

Fulgrim looked at him as though he were an idiot, a flash of hatred colouring his gaze. Once again Eidolon saw the blade swinging for his throat, as though it were poised to recur. *'No, Eidolon. Your broken soul sought you out alone, set a trap in the heart of your old pride, and tried to wear your skin as fine new armour all by itself. Of* course *I did.'* The daemon primarch laughed and slid forward, reaching out with the tip of the blade. He pressed it just below Eidolon's throat. *'The Warmaster's plans take time. Waiting is a tedious conceit. I made my own amusement. It was a paltry thing to snatch it from the warp and bend it to my will. Draw it here to a place resonant in your soul and memory... Such fun.'*

'All this just to keep you from becoming bored.' Eidolon shook his head. 'A waste. I hope you're pleased with yourself.'

'Sometimes,' Fulgrim admitted, *'I even impress myself. More and more since Iydris. New gifts and new glories. Yet crafting this diversion was most entertaining, sweet Eidolon.'*

'And what do you want from me, father? Congratulations for a game well played?'

'Perhaps I simply wished to see you made whole, or at the very least rendered interesting.' Fulgrim glanced at the small knot of warriors, hunched beneath the clipped edges of the pit. Bloody runoff had begun to drizzle down from above in a gory waterfall. *'Or wished to see if the Third Millennial were truly in good hands. You do so enjoy thinking of yourself as my successor...'*

The primarch walked and yet Eidolon heard the scraping of scales against stone, the mutilated reality in which the primarch's snake body writhed across the ground insinuating itself bit by bit. 'You are a fool,' Eidolon said finally.

The primarch rippled with joyous cackling, the sound pouring from him in an echoing wave. *'Oh, a fool, is it! Perhaps I carved away your head too soon, Eidolon. I should have kept you at my side. As a naysmith as my brother maintained. As though you would ever second-guess anything I ever said.'* One immaculate gauntlet rose and tapped against his lower lip, thoughtfully. *'That being said, you questioning me is why I took your head in the first place.'*

'Sorry to disappoint you,' he snarled through gritted teeth.

'Now that, *you never fail at.'*

'I am made in your image,' Eidolon said. 'Shaped by your teachings and your failings.'

'Ahh, of course you blame me for your mistakes.' The others had risen and gathered around them as they spoke, keeping a respectful distance. Eidolon imagined there were few who would dare the primarch's wrath as he was now. *'I offered you a rare gift, Eidolon. An opportunity to be made whole and to seize greatness.'* The primarch hooked a taloned finger into the skin of Eidolon's face and dragged it through his flesh.

Eidolon hissed at the sudden rush of pleasure and pain, the sensation of the blood dappling down his cheek and armoured shoulder. He leant into it. He would not be humbled. He forced his face against the bladed digit and let it bite. Eidolon could feel it pushing deeper, scraping against the bone.

Pain could be overcome in the pursuit of perfection. That was what he had always believed and followed.

'I have greatness enough already,' Eidolon said. The blade pressed in at his throat and he ignored it. He reached up and seized Fulgrim's wrist. Eidolon felt the power within his flesh, the barely contained fury of the immaterium. It called to him with all the seductive promise that his broken soul had offered, whispering the same honeyed promises.

Fulgrim was no different to any other child of the warp. All their power was poisoned. There was strength in being mortal.

He pulled Fulgrim's arm away and watched that perfect gaze widen. Shock and admiration flickered across the primarch's flawless features before settling into a bemused sneer. *'Perhaps you do, my son.'*

Fulgrim spread his arms and a light mewling escaped his lips as he shook Eidolon's grip free. He *stretched* and his flesh and armour began to run and shift like clay. That captive light bled out of him, weeping through his transforming skin. Fulgrim reared up as his abdomen distended and more arms forced their way through skin and ceramite, clawing at the air. His tail whipped about behind him before it coiled forwards, winding around Eidolon as the daemon primarch drew ever nearer.

His eyes were pools of black fire where dying stars wheeled and collided. Fulgrim's beauty was an atrocity in itself. It was horror shaped into art. He was the most beautiful and terrible thing Eidolon had ever gazed upon. Even more so than upon Iydris, perhaps more than at the Dark Triumph at Ullanor, Fulgrim now truly inhabited his Apotheosis.

'Strength is not enough, lord commander,' Fulgrim whispered. He squeezed. The slightest flex or contraction and Eidolon knew his legs would break. *'Not alone. We will not win the wars to come simply by being strongest. Our wars will be won because we are better. We shall make war in such glory and splendour that it shall burn simply to look upon us. Upon Terra's soil we shall be reborn in truth. The Emperor's Children shall come home at last, tear him from his tower, and break him underfoot.'*

'Yet we squander our resources–'

'No, Eidolon. I spend the lives of my Legion as I see fit. What are a few more bodies in the ground when you are, as a whole, sharper now than you were before?' Two of Fulgrim's arms grasped Eidolon by the arms and another two braced against his breastplate. *'You feel it, do you not? Rising from the ashes of your soul and taking wing. I have given that gift to you, my son. New strength and determination.'*

'You think this is a gift? You would have made me into a

mere thing of the warp – your lesser and your shadow – had I
not chosen another path.'

Fulgrim smirked. *'Oh, I cared not which side triumphed. Be
you bound by flesh or ascendant in spirit, it would have brought
me much amusement.'*

'All the more reason for me to set my own fate. If our fathers
are uncaring, all the better to spite them.'

'You always were a contrary child,' Fulgrim tutted. The daemon
primarch shook his head and his black eyes flared suddenly
with disappointed anger. *'Have I cultivated too much wasted
potential? Sons who never lived up to my expectations? Perhaps
I should have tried harder to shepherd you all to your destinies.
Or simply skinned more of you alive and made my throne from
your bones. Hmm?'*

Eidolon shook his head. 'Your capriciousness did not leave
you when you ascended, father. No. Far from it. Your mercurial
paranoia and desperation for approval have only accelerated,
fuelled and fattened by the warp. It has seeped into your heart
and swelled the gardens of your own failings – crops of venal
pettiness and fickle madness, filled to bursting by the sea of
souls!'

The mania passed as readily as it had come. One of Fulgrim's
hands drifted up to stroke along Eidolon's unmarred cheek. He
wore no gauntlets, but the passage of the clawed fingers left lines
of fire down Eidolon's skin, as potent as a power-fielded claw.
Rippling electrostatic aftershocks trickled through his flesh,
setting the nerves ablaze and making his face twitch and tic.

'Perhaps…' Eidolon forced the words out. 'We are all the
products of fathers who cared too little until it was too late.'

Fulgrim's hand snapped up and seized Eidolon's hair, yank-
ing his head back with such fury that vertebrae ground against
one another. Eidolon hissed with pain. The primarch didn't
flinch, instead leaning closer to savour the discharge of power.

'*Impressive…*' he whispered, so close that only Eidolon could hear him. The Lord Commander Primus' eyes snapped from side to side, trying to look anywhere but at the burning incarnation of the Dark Prince's might. All around them the Third Millennial had closed in. None knew what to do. Weapons were held ready, but to what end? He could see the conflict warring within them. Slaves to two masters. Some of the warriors had their eyes locked on the floor. Unable or unwilling to regard Fulgrim in his true form.

'*Look at me. Look at me!*' the primarch snapped as he shook Eidolon. Eidolon's eyes focused back upon him. A forked purple tongue slid from between Fulgrim's lips. '*Excellent. You are capable of listening, then. Yet so disobedient and wilful. You've never forgiven me, have you?*'

'I–'

'*Don't deny it!*' Fulgrim snarled. '*I have given you such gifts, Eidolon. Such opportunities. Why do you spurn me? You could not escape me. I bear a father's love and a father's failings. I do not deny this… But I will not suffer your mewling disdain. Not here. Not now. Terra is before us. Terra! There will be no greater conflict. No truer moment nor opportunity than when we have the Throneworld's throat beneath our boot. My father's precious Palace laid bare and broken. Imagine the opportunity there, to see him brought low and broken.*'

'I will be there,' Eidolon panted as he kicked out. Fulgrim lifted him bodily and let the blows rain against his breastplate and undulating flesh. The coils tightened and Fulgrim grinned.

'*If I allow it,*' he sneered. '*If you forgive me. I took your life and I had Fabius give it back. I was the lash and the rod at your back, and now look at you, my son. You held a third of the Legion to task. You ran down the Khan and his savages. You were the first to come to me at Ullanor when I called upon my sons. Now all I ask is that you forgive, and serve.*'

'You killed me!' Eidolon snapped. His voice boomed off the unnaturally smooth walls and staggered the gathering knot of warriors. Fulgrim barely flinched. The primarch's baleful radiance flared. The unclean light caught upon stray pools of blood, making the crimson fluid writhe with gaudy illumination. Shapes moved within them, faces pressing up as though against window glass. Impossible breath fogged the veil between worlds, taunted forth by their master, drawn so very close to be his handmaids or confidants.

Eidolon tasted the stink of the Phoenician. Drank it in, through his nose and mouth, every last pore opening to absorb the pheromone reek of the demigod. In their mortal existence even the least of the primarchs had possessed a power that could unman all but the strongest of warriors. Often strength of will had been all that saved a man from being reduced to a babbling imbecile.

Fulgrim was swollen with venomous charisma. It radiated from him in an almost physical wave. It would have driven Eidolon away had he not been held in place, pinned like a specimen, burning beneath the lamplight of his father's attention and affection.

'You killed me,' Eidolon repeated, his voice low and quaking. 'On a whim. For nothing.'

'I had you brought back…'

'As an afterthought! Yet more of your fickleness and vanity!' Eidolon's throat pulsed with sympathetic anger, and he reached up, seizing hold of Fulgrim's grasping arms and forcing them back. He dropped, hitting the ground, almost going to his knees. Eidolon surged up as his throat aligned and dilated.

The scream erupted from him, forced out and hurled against his master. It was near volcanic in its fury, a pyroclastic body blow that drove the primarch back. Flesh struck stone with a wet, hissing slap. The daemon's tail flailed through the air even as his torso slid back upright, leaving an acid smear like a slug's trail behind him.

'I am not your slave or your puppet,' Eidolon snarled. His hand closed around the discarded haft of *Glory Aeterna* and swept the weapon up. It swung in a hissing arc of discharged lightning, trailing it like the tails of a comet. Fulgrim slithered out of the way, his body going flat against the ground as the hammer slammed into the stonework, gouging a fresh crater.

'And look at you now. A man of your own will. A soldier of intent.' Fulgrim ducked and dodged a second and a third attack, and then brought his hands up. Swords shimmered into being, their gilded edges catching the next strike, turning it aside. A storm of slashes rained down upon Eidolon, an intricate pattern of blows that each missed him, pinning him between a web of sword blades, trapping him against the wall and ground. The blades flexed barely a micron and Eidolon hissed. Pain saturated him till his nerves sang and blood ran from the barely perceptible wounds in his plate and flesh.

'You cannot imagine,' Fulgrim said, and drew himself closer still. Close enough that Eidolon could smell the sugar-and-cyanide odour of his breath. *'I could be a beautiful death if you so desire. At my hand you could cross that veil once more and be mere prey for those who wait beyond. My beloved N'kari is there, and my master's favoured handmaiden. All those who serve the will and want of the Dark Prince would have their turn with you, my sweet Eidolon. What will your answer be?'*

One of the swords, a silver blade with its hilt entwined by carved writhing bodies, evaporated in a hiss of opiate smoke. Fulgrim's clawed hand shot forward and seized Eidolon's chin, forcing him to look directly into the piteous eyes. He could see the madness and desperation screaming there, flickering around the barest memory of the man Fulgrim had been, before the monstrosity of his vice and ego had subsumed him forever.

'I will lead my men as I always have,' Eidolon said at last. 'I will lead them to Terra itself and I will do it for myself alone. For the glory that is due to me.'

'Was that so difficult?' Fulgrim laughed. He flung his many arms wide, each one poised at a different angle, an ancient avatar of divinity given new life and potency. *'Once perhaps I might have kept you alive merely because it pleased me, Eidolon, but you have wrought a wonder here – that much is true.'* Fulgrim spun about and turned his attention outwards. Almost as one the gathered warriors sank to their knees. There was little other choice in the face of it, the storm of Fulgrim's love, the air cut by the knives of his fickle affections. Only the Kakophoni remained standing, priming their weapons.

'Sons of the Third Legion. Children of the Emperor. Hear me! Your master calls!

'You have fought and bled for me, and I love each of you for your service. Just as I cherish the service of your Lord Commander Primus.' He paused as though mulling over Eidolon's full, and self-given, title, before continuing. *'He has struggled on your behalf, led boldly and bravely. He pleases me, just as your service has pleased him!'* Mischief danced in Fulgrim's dark eyes.

Somehow it did not matter that he was now a warp-swollen monster, a looming and many-armed serpent god; Fulgrim commanded their attention as readily as he had on the parade ground or as they were poised to swear an oath of moment.

'My son,' Fulgrim murmured as he slithered forwards, arms reaching out in one motion to seize Eidolon, as though in some conspiratorial embrace. His sharply angled face slid next to Eidolon's, his lips at the Lord Commander Primus' ear. *'This is the last time you disobey me. You have grown strong and proud, but next to me you are still nothing.'* Fulgrim's hands clenched and caressed, some drifting across the plates of Eidolon's armour where others held him fiercely. With but a gesture

he could rip Eidolon limb from limb. *'Try my patience again and your great sacrifice will be in vain. Not even the Dark Prince will protect you from my wrath.'*

Fulgrim pushed himself away and turned from Eidolon, arms upraised. Black lightning coursed along the vanes of his outstretched limbs as he lifted skyward, haloed by violet flame. The primarch's physical shell broke apart, becoming a rain of gold, a flutter of rose petals, a sudden rush of perfumed air. All eyes followed his ascent and dissolution. A moment of silence passed, in wonderful fragility.

Eidolon allowed himself a moment of peace. He cast his eyes heavenward, through the pall of Fulgrim's ascent. Far above, through the nest of tortured masonry and ruined catacombs, he could see the first hints of light.

'He is not wrong,' Eidolon said at last. The others looked at him, still shell-shocked from the passage of the primarch, trying in vain to tear their gaze from Fulgrim's wake. 'We have all suffered here, brothers. We have become the playthings of the warp, rather than its masters. The gods are fickle and so the primarch has grown yet more fickle.' He laughed bitterly, walking across the centre of the chamber, surveying the warriors under his command.

His warriors. His Millennial. His Legion.

There was no shame now. The primarch could not humble him. Whatever pain he had felt had passed, washed away in the double-edged euphoria that came with Fulgrim's presence. There would only be Terra, after this. No more distractions or games. Only the final test.

'We have been tested, but we have not been found wanting,' he went on, turning *Glory Aeterna* over and over again as he did so. 'This wretched world burns. Our enemies are routed. Our superiority is undeniable. Others can claim their ascendancy, prostitute the name of their primarch, hold rank over us as though it matters. We have proved them wrong.' He reached down and scooped up a handful of ashes.

'There will come a time when we are free to indulge our desires, to carve our wants across a galaxy that belongs to the strong.' He let the detritus of the world, of its people, of the Sons of Horus, drift through his fingers. 'On that day, I shall lead us out, and not even the gods themselves shall cease our revels.'

Cheers greeted his pronouncements. Eidolon grinned his slack grin.

'Hail the Lord Commander Primus!' Vocipheron called. Others took up the cry. Malakris whooped and jeered, his vigour temporarily surging. Plegua and the other Kakophoni resumed their song once more.

'Come,' Eidolon said as the others gathered about him, at last looking heavenward with fresh eyes, their souls soaring like the phoenix itself reborn. 'We have a long road ahead of us.'

ACKNOWLEDGEMENTS

A character of this gravitas, a truly iconic villain of the Heresy, cannot be borne alone. Many pairs of hands contributed to this book being what it is.

I would like to thank Jacob Youngs for his constant support and advice, for making this book as good as it could possibly be. I'd also like to thank Chris Wraight for his advice on how to handle the character and what makes him tick. You were a lifesaver.

For my wife, Anne-Sophie, for all of her support during the struggles. For my hobby group – Gareth, Mark-Anthony, Chris, Daniel, James and Sean – for always pushing me to be a better writer. I'd like to thank Dylan and Sebastian for the inspiration that your opposing appreciations of the III Legion have always provided.

Finally, I would like to thank everyone who has contributed to the mythos of Eidolon and the Emperor's Children: Graham McNeill, Josh Reynolds, Mike Haspil and Chris Wraight. You have made my research pile an absolutely exquisite pleasure to peruse.

ABOUT THE AUTHOR

Marc Collins is a speculative fiction author living and working in Glasgow, Scotland. He is the writer of the Warhammer Crime novel *Grim Repast,* as well as the short story 'Cold Cases', which featured in the anthology *No Good Men.* For Warhammer 40,000 he has written the novels *Void King, Helbrecht: Knight of the Throne* and the Dawn of Fire novel *The Martyr's Tomb.* When not dreaming of the far future he works in Pathology with the NHS.

VALDOR: BIRTH OF THE IMPERIUM
by Chris Wraight

Constantin Valdor is the chief of the Emperor's Custodian Guard and among the closest of His companions. As the wars of Unity come to their end, he faces his greatest challenge, as dark deeds are required to pave mankind's road to the stars.

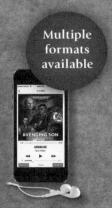

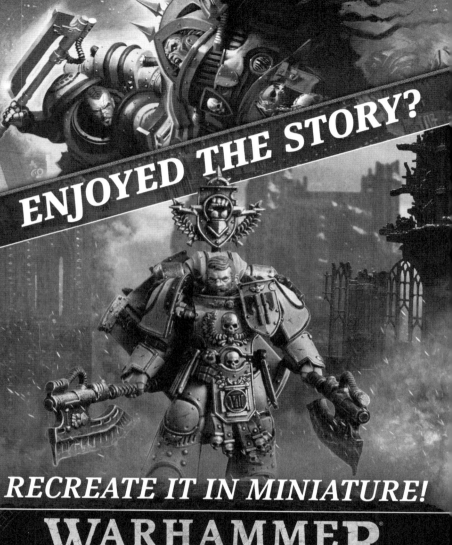